Len Ellsworth Tilden

The Stolen Will

A comedy drama, in three acts

Len Ellsworth Tilden

The Stolen Will
A comedy drama, in three acts

ISBN/EAN: 9783744781657

Printed in Europe, USA, Canada, Australia, Japan

Cover: Foto ©Andreas Hilbeck / pixelio.de

More available books at **www.hansebooks.com**

THE

STOLEN WILL.

A COMEDY. DRAMA,

IN THREE ACTS.

BY LEN ELLSWORTH TILDEN, "INK."

Respectfully dedicated, by the Author, to the Marlborough
Dramatic Club, who successfully presented it
the first time it was produced, at
Marlborough, N. H.,
May 20, 1881.

SYNOPSIS.

A Description of the Costumes. Cast of Characters. Entrances and Exits. Properties. Stage
Directions.

MARLBORO', N. H.:
PUBLISHED BY THE AUTHOR.
1881.

THE

STOLEN WILL.

A COMEDY DRAMA,

IN THREE ACTS.

BY LEN ELLSWORTH TILDEN, "INK."

Respectfully dedicated, by the Author, to the Marlborough
Dramatic Club, who successfully presented it
the first time it was produced, at
Marlborough, N. H.,
May 20, 1881.

SYNOPSIS.

A Description of the Costumes. Cast of Characters. Entrances and Exits. Properties. Stage
Directions.

MARLBORO', N. H.:
PUBLISHED BY THE AUTHOL..
1881.

CAST OF CHARACTERS.

The cast is here given with the names of those who were first cast to present the play.

CORONER, an old Magistrate.................................JAIRUS COLLINS
CHIP WINKLE, Esq., a long, lank, country Boy.........FRED. E. McINTYRE
Master MARKEY LOKER, an overgrown Booby.......GEO. K. HARRINGTON
GEO. JAMESON, a Villain....................................FRANK H. McINTYRE
AMOS WENLEY, an old Farmer......................... ⎫
DEACON CUFF, Deacon of the Orthodox Church, and ⎬ FRANK H. PEASLEE
   President of the town Reform Club................. ⎭
Hon. EDWARD ENWRIGHT, a Foreign Traveller........CLINTON COLLINS
TOMMY SAUNDERS, smart and saucy.....................EDDIE M. TENNEY
POLICE, an Officer that takes care of Children................HARRY CLARK
FOOTMAN, one of Old England's class...................HARRY A. TENNEY
SHERIFF, an Officer with a Badge......................... ⎫
COP, one of the finest Police in the world............. . ⎬ HENRY L. BRYANT
VIOLA WENLEY, a Child of Adoption...........Miss FLORA M. BLODGETT
SARAH LOKER, a Society Belle ....Miss MINNIE BARKER
MADAM LOKER, a Lady of the Period..........Miss LILLA M. KNOWLTON
LITTLE CORA, an only Child.............................Miss BELLE TENNEY
BETSEY SMITH, a bold, bad Woman.................Mrs. CARRIE L. FITCH
KATHLEEN, a Nurse Girl..................................Miss MAY TENNEY
     Citizens, Firemen, Newsboy and Constable by Members of the Club.

Master Marky Loker and the Police, an officer who takes care of children, are burlesque characters. The former must be played by as large a person as can be got, and the latter by a very small boy.

SYNOPSIS.

ACT I.—Viola's arrival home from school. Tells about a dark featured man. Appearance of Chip Winkle, Esq., who's right from Wildland. Betsey Smith says he's a fool. Chip agrees with her. Amos Wenley concludes to keep him and he is bound out to him until he is of age. George Jameson demands his daughter. Murder of Amos Wenley. Betsey Smith steals the will. The coroner takes charge of Wenley Farm. Chip is disgusted with things. Betsey Smith turns Viola out of house and home. Farewell scene between Viola and Chip. Tommy Saunders and Chip talk the matter over. Chip sees Betsey Smith have the stolen will and steals it from her. Deacon Cuff and Betsey are excited. Potato bugs and whiskey. The Deacon and Betsey go to town. Chip Winkle, Esq., is bound for New York with the stolen will. "Good bye until Viola is found."

ACT II.—Madam Loker and daughter talk about George Jameson and the Hon. Edward Enwright. Arrival of Viola, who is engaged as governess. Dr. Merriam says that Marky is prematurely developed mentally. Marky cries because

Kathleen won't rock him. Appearance of Jameson. Marky talks French. School room scene. Viola drills the pupils. Cora and Marky speak a piece. Chip's arrival in New York. " Mighty big town, New York." Chip has an adventure with a Cop. " That thing in your mouth is red-hot and smoke is pouring right out of you!" Viola, Cora and Marky out walking. Marky gets lost. Chip gets on track of Viola. Madam is worried because Cora takes to the governess so. Sarah laughs at Madam's fears. Arrival of Enwright from Europe. Cora tells about the governess. Enwright's account of his foreign tour. Madam thinks he is somewhat changed. Sarah agrees with madam. " Beauty will never win him." Meeting of Enwright and Viola. Marky gives Madam away bad. Jameson alone in the parlor of the Loker mansion. Chip blunders in, searching for Viola. Chip tells about the stolen will. Jameson says that he is Viola's friend and will keep the will until her return, so it will not get lost. Chip finally consents to it and leaves. Jameson kidnaps Viola and Cora. " Now for a fortune." Chip is disgusted with New York. He cannot find Viola or Jameson. Gets an old paper stuck on to him by a newsboy. Reads that Viola has stolen little Cora, as it's supposed. Gets mad. Meets Enwright. Gets track of Jameson. Enwright looking for Chip.

ACT III.—Cora and Viola in prison. Jameson enters and tells them why they are locked up. " It's for money, yes, money." Jameson produces the stolen will. " It's father's will, willing his property to me, his adopted daughter." Jameson proves that he is Viola's father. Jameson and Chip up in New Hampshire. Jameson is drunk. Chip gets the will. Fire! fire! fire! The Deacon and Betsey. Popping the question. Old Maccaboy raises the old boy. Enwright, Viola, Cora and Chip at Wenley farm. Betsey is scared. " The Lord save us! It's Viola and Chip." Chip produces the stolen will. " I stole it back from Jameson." Betsey is going to kill herself. Chip thinks her funeral procession will not be very long. Death of Jameson. Enwright announces the engagement of himself and Viola. " Well, I'll be gol darned. Who would have thought all this would have happened just because of the ' Stolen Will '."

COSTUMES.

CORONER COLLINS. Act I. Scene 1 : Swallow-tail coat, old fashioned tall hat, cane and glasses ; rest of suit to correspond.

CHIP WINKLE, ESQ. Act I. Scenes 1, 2 and 3 : Ragged pants, strapped up by one gallows ; checked shirt, old straw hat ; barefoot, one toe done up with rag ; long light-haired wig. Act II. Scene 3. Act III. Scenes 2, 3 and 4 : Short waisted coat, short legged pants, an old stiff hat, large shoes, red handkerchief around neck. Wig as in Act I.

MASTER MARKY LOKER. Act II. Scenes 1 and 2 : Knee pants cut long waisted, frock cut short waisted, ruffle around throat, copper-toed shoes. Act II. Scene 3 : The same as in the two above scenes, excepting the addition of a small straw hat.

GEORGE JAMESON. Act I. Scene 1 : Showy walking suit. Act II. Scenes 1, 2 and 4 : Dress suit. Act III. Scene 1 : Light gray suit, slouch hat, low necked sailor's shirt, pants tucked into high legged boots. Act III. Scene 2 : Traveling suit. Act III. Scene 4 : Pants and vest ; bareheaded ; appearances indicating that he has been through a fire.

AMOS WENLEY. Act I. Scene 1 : Homespun suit of gray, straw hat, bald headed wig.

DEACON CUFF. Act I. Scene 3 : Act III. Scenes 3 and 4 : Linen duster, checked vest, black pants, tall hat, standing collar, with black necktie, large red. handkerchief, gray haired wig.

HON. EDWARD ENWRIGHT. Act II. Scene 4 : Act III. Scenes 2, 3 and 4 : Fashionable traveling suit and cane.

TOMMY SAUNDERS. Act 1. Scene 2 : Boy's suit, home-made ; straw hat.

NEWSBOY. Act III. Scene 2 : Ragged rig ; barefooted.

POLICE. Act II. Scene 3 : Policeman's suit and badge.

FOOTMAN. Act III. Scenes 1 and 4 : Long dress coat of black, pants of same color, white vest and gloves, large watch chain, standing collar, red necktie.

SHERIFF. Act III. Scene 4 : Citizen's clothes ; large badge.

COP. Act II. Scene 3 : Regular New York police style.

VIOLA WENLEY. Act I. Scenes 1, 2 and 4 : Act II. Scene 1 : Plain but neat traveling suit. Act II. Scene 2 : Light summer dress. Act II. Scene 3: Walking suit. Act III. Scene 1: Dark dress. Act III. Scene 4: Dark dress and waterproof.

SARAH LOKER. Act II. Scenes 1, 2 and 4: Stylish evening dress of light.

MADAM LOKER. Act II. Scenes 1, 2 and 4. Stylish evening dress of dark.

LITTLE CORA. Act II. Scene 2: Light summer dress. Act II. Scenes 3 and 4: White dress and hat, white kid shoes. Act III. Scene 1: Light summer dress. Act III. Scene 4: Light summer dress and waterproof.

BETSEY SMITH. Act I. Scenes 1, 2 and 3: Act III. Scene 4: Checked dress, white apron. glasses, cap, hair combed down over ears. In last part Act I, Scene 3. add an old bonnet and shawl.

KATHLEEN. Act II. Scene 1: Plain gown, handkerchief tied over head in turban style.

CONSTABLE. Act III. Scene 3: Citizen's suit and badge.

CITIZENS AND FIREMEN. Act III. Scene 3: Citizens and Firemen's suits.

PROPERTIES.

Settee, kitchen table with drawer, five common chairs, parlor table. three parlor chairs, organ, a will, a marriage certificate, stocking of silver, a paper of authority, dirk and revolver, pen and ink, cigar, pails. hoes and shovels, police badges, rag baby, wheelbarrow, two fans, two canes, two jack-knives. bundle done up in a red handkerchief slung on a stick. trunk, red and green fire powder with arrangements for burning the same, small stone, five-foot ladder with short distance between rounds, bundle of newspapers. pint whiskey bottle, snuff box. supper dishes, food and drink, market basket, with vegetables and eggs, churn, tray of mince meat and chopping knife, pillow, globe, maps and books.

STAGE DIRECTIONS.

(Actors supposed to be on stage facing audience.)

Exits and Entrances.—R. means right; L. left; 1 E. 1st entrance; 2 E. 2d entrance; 3 E. 3d entrance.

Relatives Position on Stage.—R. means right; C. centre; L. left.

Plan of Scenes.—Front Curtain; Street Scene; Forest Scene; Parlor Scene; Chamber Prison Scene; Kitchen Scene; School Room Scene. The scenes are so arranged that they can be run without letting down the front curtain, except between acts.

Time of presentation of drama two hours and a half.

THE STOLEN WILL.

ACT I.

Scene First.—Kitchen. Four chairs, table, settee. Amos Wenley on settee asleep. Betsey Smith sweeping.

Amos. (Muttering in his sleep.) Viola!

Bestey. All men are fools, yes, fools, and Amos Wenley especially. Here he is asleep on the settee and a mutturing "Viola." Plague take her, I say. Before her advent I was sure of being left all the property, but now my cake is dough, yes, dough, and doughed by that Viola Wenley. Now she is coming home from school and with her coming things will be worse than ever, for I can't bear the sight of her. She is nobody but the brat of that jade of a Mary Fernald, who crawled back here to die after having promised to marry that fool of an Amos, and then run off with that villian of George Jameson, who deserted her in a short time. To think that she should come back here and that Amos Wenley should adopt her child, giving the brat the family name, and that he should bring the hussey up a lady! Bah! (Takes a pinch of snuff.) I have kept house for him ever since the old folks died and the property should be mine. It shall be, too!

Amos. (Waking up and going to door.) Eh? Betsey, didn't you hear the stage coming? I thought I heard the sound of the wheels.

Betsey. (Aside.) Awake or asleep, all he thinks of is that girl. (Addressing Amos.) I was not minding, but it is about time for it.

Amos. Yes, I heard it, for here it is.

Viola. (Coming in at door.) And here am I, father dear, home again to stay. (Hugs and kisses Amos, and turns to Betsey.) Ah, Betsey, I am glad to see you again, and looking so well too. With my help things shall be easier for you hereafter.   [Betsey coldly bows.

Amos. Viola, how you have grown! You are as handsome as a picture. I shall have to look out or some young fellow will be taking you from me.

Betsey. (Aside in a sneering tone.) "Father dear!" "With my help!" "Handsome as a picture!" Fiddlesticks. (Addressing Viola.) Well, I suppose you want to change your gown. You will find your old room ready for you.

VIOLA. Thank you, I should. Father, will you please go down to the gate and get my trunk for me.

AMOS. Certainly, at once.

[Exit Amos at door, Viola L. 2 E.

BETSEY. A pretty kittle of fish, I declare; but this won't do for me, for I've got supper to get.

[Enter Amos at door, exit L. 2 E. Betsey sets table for supper. Enter Amos L. 2 E.

AMOS. Well, Betsey, Viola has grown to be a nice young lady, hasn't she?

BETSEY. Nice enough.

AMOS. Why do you speak so?

BETSEY. Because, Amos Wenley, I think it is all nonsense for you to do as you are doing by that gal. She don't deserve it.

AMOS. (Excited.) Betsey Smith, don't you ever let me hear you speak so of Viola again. (Fetching his hand down on to the table.) Remember it!

BESTEY. (Aside). How the old fool flares up.

[Enter Viola L. 2 E.

VIOLA. How nice to be at home again!

BETSEY. Supper is ready. [All sit down at table.

AMOS. Now, Viola, you must tell us all about yourself.

VIOLA. There is not much to add to what I have written, excepting that a dark complected man has followed me several times lately, and I do not know what to make of it. I have got rid of him though, without doubt, by coming home.

BETSEY. (Aside.) He probably thought she was on the "pick up,"—nothing strange at all.

AMOS. (Aside.) Can it be George Jameson? (Addressing Viola.) It is strange, but you have probably seen the last of him.

VIOLA. I hope so. [Knock at the door.

AMOS. Come in. [Enter Chip Winkle, Esq., at door.

AMOS. Well, what do you want?

CHIP. I want to let out. Don't ye want to hire?

AMOS. Well, my boy, I don't know as I do. Where'd you come from? (Pause.) Come, come, speak up.

CHIP. He! he! (Points with his finger out at window.) He! he! he! Run away from over there, sir. I did by vum! Been livin' there. Couldn't keep me any longer; nobody stops. I wouldn't either. Made me work like a nigger, pick taters, pull weeds; starve everybody over there; guess they won't ever ketch me again.

BETSEY. A pauper run away from the Wildland poor house, most likely.

Amos. So I reckon. They do work them like slaves over there, children and all, I have heard said; almost starving them into the bargain. Poor boy! give him some supper; he looks as though he had not eaten anything for a week. Set a plate for him, Betsey.

[Betsey sets a plate and places a chair for him.

Amos. Come, sit up and help yourself—Tom, Dick, Harry —What's your name?

[Chip throws hat down and sits down and eats.

Chip. My name! Chip, Chip Winkle. I likes it the best the way Henry Mason writes it at school with a tail to it, E–s–q., that's for Squire, ye know, same as Squire Converse spells his'n.

Betsey. (Holding up her hands.) The Lord save us! He's a half wit.

Chip. (Cramming stuff into his mouth and looking at Betsey.) Who be ye? Hah?

Betsey. Who be I? I am Betsey Smith, you fool.

Chip. Funny name Smith.

Betsey. (Threateningly). Shet up! (In a surprised tone.) Gracious, how he eats.

[All shove back from the table but Chip.

Chip. (Pointing to Viola.) Say, Mister, am she an angel? [Viola laughs, Betsey looks cross, Amos smiles.

Amos. No, but worthy to be. What made you ask such a question, Chip?

Chip. Oh, becuz I seed a picter of one in old Granny White's Bible, once, and she looks just like it, so kind of white and soft, like cotton and wool, but if she ain't an angel she is pretty nigh one, I vum. (Getting up from table.) That's good! cornprime! Most I have eat for a month. (Points.) Couldn't get so much over there.

Amos. I don't know but what I'll hire you, after all.

Betsey. For gracious sakes, what are you thinking of, Amos Wenley? Why, he will be more plague than profit.

Chip. Just what they said over there, ma'am. (Points.) That's just what they said every day.

Amos. I have taken quite a fancy to the lad. He seems willing and handy, and I need somebody to do the chores. What is your opinion, Viola?

Viola. I should keep him. He's been neglected and ill-treated, that's evident enough.

Betsey. (Aside, taking a pinch of snuff.) That settles it.

Amos. Well, well, let us talk about business. What can you do to make yourself useful, Chip?

Chip. (In a high key.) Hey?

2

Amos. What can you do?

Chip. (Brightens up.) Why, I cuts wood, fetches water, feeds the pigs, drives the cows and does lots of everything. Done heaps over there. (Points) 'Twas "Chip, come here," and " Run, you lazy dog," and " Scoot, you nigger," and so at last I ups and runs away. Couldn't stand so much, ye see.

Betsey. (Clearing off table.) He's a fool and such a looking object. Ugh, how he looks!

Chip. (Grinning and eyeing Betsey.) Ma'am, " Handsome is that handsome does," so old Granny White says. Don't look very nice now, but can slick up ye know. This ere hat ain't my Sunday-go-to-meeting one; got a new straw one over there. (Points.) Left it though.

[Amos and Viola laugh. Betsey scowls.

Amos. We will let him stay and I'll ride over to Wildland poor farm tomorrow, and if he belongs there get him bound out to me. They are overrun with paupers and will be glad enough to get one off their hands I reckon. (Gets his hat.) But come, my lad; come out doors. I want to see how smart you are.

[Exit Amos and Chip at door, putting on hats.

Viola. (Addressing Betsey.) Is there anything I can do to help you?

Betsey. (Sullenly.) No.

Viola. (Going out L. 2 E.) Well, then I will go to my room and arrange my things.

Betsey. What this place is coming to is more than I can tell. First a stuck up hussey of a girl is taken in, and now he has got a fool. The Lord only knows what he will be up to next. Plague take it all!

[Exit Betsey R. 2. E. Enter Amos at door.

Amos. Well, John Logan, overseer of the Wildland poor-farm, has bound Chip Winkle, Esq., to me until he becomes of age. How scared Chip was when he saw Logan coming. Poor boy! This man that followed Viola troubles me; can it be Jameson? I pray not. Viola looks upon me as a father, and does not know that he is alive. She is as a daughter to me, and all I have shall be hers when I die. But this man! Who is he and what can he want?

[Enter George Jameson at door.

Jameson. He is George Jameson and he wants his daughter, yes, he demands her.

Amos. (Excited.) You villain!

Jameson. Quite complimentary!

Amos. Get out of here!

Jameson. Not until you produce my daughter.

AMOS. (More excited than ever.) George Jameson, you low lived villian, how dare you show yourself here after ruining as pure and holy a girl as ever lived, Mary Fernald. You murderer! For your desertion was the death of her. Before I would give Viola up to you I would die. A great deal you think of her. Seventeen long years have passed since Mary's death and Viola's birth, and you have not been near. Now you appear, prompted without doubt by some hellish designs. Better far to lay her in the grave than give her over to you.

JAMESON. Tut, tut, old man, be careful. The law gives her to me, and I shall take her.

AMOS. By the God's you shall not, Leave this house instantly.

JAMESON. Don't get excited.

AMOS. Leave!

[Amos rushes at Jameson. They clasp and struggle. Jameson draws dirk and stabs Amos, who falls to stage with a scream.

JAMESON. (Looking about in a frightened manner.) The old fool! I only wanted him to think I was going to take the girl so as to get a stake out of him. But blast it, I must get out of this before I get caught.

[Exit Jameson at door in haste.

Amos. (Groaning.) I am done for. Stabbed to death by Viola's father. For her sake he shall escape. I'll never tell who did it, for Betsey knows that Jameson is her father.

[Enter Chip at door. Viola L. 2 E. Betsey R. 2 E. All excited.

ALL THREE. What's the matter?

AMOS. (Low.) I am stabbed. Get me on to the settee.

[They put him onto the settee, Viola arranging pillow.

VIOLA. Oh, father, you bleed awfully. (Holds handkerchief to wound.) How did it happen?

AMOS. (Gasping.) A man came in; we had a dispute and it led to a fight. He struck me with a knife. I am dying, dying. Viola, sing to me, sing that beautiful song "Eternity Dawns."

[Viola, resting his head on her arm, mournfully sings, "Eternity Dawns." Tune No. 278 of Gospel Hymns combined.

"Eternity dawns on my vision to-day;
Gather round me, my loved ones, to sing and to pray.
The shadows are past and the veil is withdrawn;
Brightly now does the morn of eternity dawn.

CHORUS: Hallelujah, hallelujah, hallelujah we sing,
Jesus conquered the grave, robbing death of its sting.

Hosanna ! again let the glad anthem ring.
Sing and pray. Eternity dawns.

Eternity dawns! Oh, the glories that rise,
How they burst on my soul in blissful surprise.
With rapture the gleam of the city I see,
Where the crown and the mansion are waiting for me.

CHORUS.

Eternity dawns! There will be no more night;
I am nearing the gates of the city of light.
The shadows of time are all passing away,
Tarry not, O my Saviour, come quickly I pray.

CHORUS.

Eternity dawns! Earth recedes from my view;
Weeping friends, now farewell, I must bid you adieu;
I am resting in Jesus. His merits I plead;
Fear you not for my God shall supply all your need."

CHORUS.

Amos. Eternity dawns! I come. (Falling back.) Father, I come.

Viola. Dead! Oh, my soul, he is dead. [Faints.

Betsey. What a muss! (Addressing Chip.) Here Chip, you brat, take hold and help get her to her room.

Chip. (Sobbing.) My name ain't Chip you brat. It is Chip Winkle, Esq.

Betsey. (Sneering.) Well, Mr. Chip Winkle, Esq., will you please help me get this gal up stairs.

[Exit Chip and Betsey L. 2 E. with Viola. Enter Chip and Betsey L. 2 E.

Betsey. Now run and get Coroner Collins. Start your boots. [Exit Chip at door.

Betsey. (Takes pinch of snuff.) Now the coast is clear. I have the old will Amos Wenley made before that Jazabel came, giving the property to me. I'll substitute it for the last one he made giving the property to Viola Wenley. The lawyer that made it is dead, and the witnesses are gone, no one knows where. The old will was made by Squire Converse up here, and the witnesses are all a-living. Betsey Smith, you are all right. Now for his bed-room where he keeps the will. [Exit Betsey R. 1 E. ; enter same with will.

Betsey. The deed is done! Shall I burn the will? No, I have not time, for here comes the coroner. (Puts will in dress.) [Enter Chip and Coroner at door.

Coroner. (Shaking hands with Betsey.) Miss Smith, I believe.

Betsey. (Low.) Yes, sir.

Coroner. (Crossing over and looking at body.) Ah. madam, a sad case, this, very sad !

Betsey. (Crying and wiping her eyes with apron.) Yes. Oh, oh, what shall I do? he was like a brother to me.

CHIP. (Aside.) How she goes it now, the old sardine. I hate her. Mighty little she cares.

CORONER. Yes, Amos was a good man. Emphatically so. How does Viola take it?

BETSEY. She is up stairs in her room. I stayed alone while Chip was gone.

CHIP. She fainted, sir; we had to carry her up. That we did, sir.

BETSEY. (Aside to Chip.) Shet up!

CORONER. I must do my solemn duty. Nothing can be done to-night except to take charge of the house. I myself will stay here, for Amos was an old friend of mine. But stop, do you know who committed the murder? Chip said all he knew was that it was a man.

BETSEY. No, we found him here. All he said was that a man came in and that they had a dispute and he was stabbed.

CORONER. A sad, strange, mysterious case.

BETSEY. Yes. Shall we stay with you?

CORONER. No, I prefer to be alone.

BETSEY. All right. Call, if you wish anything.

[Exit Betsey and Chip R. 2 E.

CORONER. A remarkable affair! Who can the murderer be? How queer the housekeeper answered me when I asked about Viola, and how mad she looked when the boy spoke. Truly this is a strange, queer case. "Murder will out" though!

FOREST DROP SCENE.

ACT I.

Scene Second. Woodland. Chip walking back and forth.

CHIP. I don't believe Betsey Smith was to have the stuff. She's an old tarnal. Property should have been Miss Viola's. Mr. Wenley was a good man and thought the world of Miss Viola. By gosh all hemlock! everything is t'other end up. Those pesky cows act worse than ever since they got to be Betsey's. Devil take her and the cows too.

[Enter Viola R. 2 E., dressed for traveling, bag in hand.

VIOLA. Why, Chip, you are wicked. You should not swear.

CHIP. Well, darn it!—that ain't swearing anyhow—I hate Betsey Smith, and I wish those plaguey critters were dead and in heaven.

VIOLA. What a boy you are, Chip! Cows don't go to Heaven when they die. They have not got any souls.

CHIP. Well, I don't know, but the plaguey critters pester me most to death. I tell ye it ain't quite so easy hunting up runaway cows. Darn 'em! when I do ketch 'em I allers talks up smart to 'em and calkalates they will remembèr it next time.

VIOLA. But do they, Chip?

CHIP. Lord, no! They are jest the worst beasts in town. It don't do an atom of good, jaw all ye can; they have got the poorest remembrances I ever seed. Now ye jest whip a dog and he'll behave like a gentleman, but the uglier you be with a cow, the uglier she is. I vum! 'tain't no use anyhow.

VIOLA. (Smiling.) Well, Chip, you do seem to have a hard time of it, but you must remember that it does no good to swear.

CHIP. Well, I won't, any more. I'll do anything you say. It'll come hard. though.

VIOLA. I am glad to hear you say you will leave off swearing, Chip, for I know you will stick to your word, as you never lie, but I am forgetting what I came for; Chip, I am going away.

CHIP. What! going off to stay?

VIOLA. Yes, I am going to New York as a teacher. Madam Spofford of Brightwood Seminary, where I graduated, got me the situation at a salary of three hundred per year. I am sorry to leave, but I am turned out, yes, ordered to leave. Betsey Smith did not think I had a place to go to when she told me she could not have me here any longer, but I expected it and was ready to leave.

CHIP. Oh, what shall I do? There won't be anything left to stay for now. It'll be terrible lonesome here after ye are gone. The old hog to turn ye out doors. She is too mean to live, she is.

VIOLA. Hush, Chip, you must not talk so. I shall come to see you sometimes—another year, perhaps. So cheer up.

CHIP. Well, "what must be will be," so old Granny White says. (Puts hand in his pocket and takes out an old pocket book tied with a string.) Miss Viola ye are going off a long ways, and will need all the money ye can get. Here is three dollars that I have saved doing odd jobs, and ye shall have it. (Hands it to Viola, who refuses to take it.) Please take it.

VIOLA. No, Chip, I have got money enough to take me to New York, and do not need it. I thank you just as much for it, for the will is as good as the deed. (Pauses and takes Bible from pocket and gives it to Chip.) Chip, here is a small present for you, a Bible with your name in it.

CHIP. Have ye spelt it with a E-s-q?

VIOLA. Yes. Always keep it, and read it, and in reading it remember Viola.

CHIP. Thank ye, thank ye, Miss Viola. (Whispers.) Here comes the old tarnal!   [Enter Betsey R. 2 E.

BETSEY. (Surprised.) Miss. I thought you had gone.

VIOLA. I have not, but I am going.

BETSEY. Well, go along then. (Pause.) You may come back on a visit sometime.

VIOLA. Betsey Smith, I would. never come back here to see you; when I come back here it must be as I have always lived here—by right—the right of adoption. Father meant it and you know it, but by some hook or crook the law gave all to you and made me a beggar! But I am going where I can earn my own bread; if you can eat yours without the sting of conscience you will be a happy woman! Yet one thing I would ask of you, be kind to Chip, treat him well; he is honest, good and faithful. Betsey Smith. good bye. (Turns to Chip and takes him by the hand.) Good bye, Chip.

CHIP. (Sobbing.) Good bye.   [Exit Viola L. 2 E.

BETSEY. (Aside.) Well, I never! What impudence! Can she know? But no! What a fool to be scared to death! She is mad, that's all! Much good the property will ever do Mary Fernald's brat now.   [Exit Betsey R. 2 E.

CHIP. (Seating himself on the ground.) This is a cur'us state of affairs. (Takes Bible and reads.) "In the beginning God created the heaven and the earth." (Pause.) Gosh darned, if it don't say he created everything; well, He must have been turning out poor work when He put Betsey Smith together. Safe enough to bet on that. (Reads.) "So God created man in his own image, in the image of God created he him; male and female created he them." Guess they got some new images to create by pretty soon after, by the diff'rent looks of folks. Anyway, it must take more than one image to make both men and women, cause they ain't nothin' alike. (Pause.) I'll be gosh darned if it ain't in black and white that He done it all—made everything in six days, and on the seventh day, rested; well, He, was a worker. He was.
                    [Enter Tommy Saunders L. 2 E.

TOM. So Viola has gone, has she, Chip?

CHIP. Yes, the old she-critter drove her off. I shall go next, but she won't drive me off, for she gets too much work out of me. It's dig, dig, all the time, jest like a nigger. It's Chip, here! and Chip, do this! and Chip, do that, ye vagabond! No rest or comfort since she got the stuff; the old dragon, I just won't hurry for her. I hate the concentrated combination of the slung together old tarnal, by vum, I do.

TOM. So does every body, Chip. (Picks up stone and throws it.) There, I wish I had hit her old gobbler, don't you? (Sitting down.) Father and Deacon Mason and Squire Boyden were talking about her up at the postoffice t'other day, and they said she treated you shamefully and hadn't no business here, either. I heard the deacon whisper, says he, kind o' low, "Depend upon it, she never come by that property honestly, for I remember that Squire Bridgewater told me in this very store, not six months before he died 'I've been making out Farmer Wenley's will, and depend upon it, the girl will fare well.'" (Lowers voice.) Yes, Chip, that's what I heard, and Mr. Woodward told, and he ought to know, for he writes for the *New Hampshire Sentinel* and *Independent Statesman* how when Amos Wenley was killed that Coroner Collins said that things were awfully mixed up, that the will was an older one than Squire Bridgewater said he had made, but as no other could be found the old one stood, and so Betsey Smith got all and Viola is turned out of house and home. Now, Chip, between you and me, I'll bet anything that Betsey knew where the will was that should have been found, and went and stole it. (Excited.) By George! she knows how all our speckled hens lay in her barn, and gets their eggs and sells 'em. Ain't that stealing, and if she will steal eggs wouldn't she have stole the will if she could have found it?

CHIP. What is a will, Tommy?

TOM. Why, don't you know, Chip? It's a paper folks get a lawyer to write for 'em to tell who is going to have their property and things when they are dead and done with it. Now, you see, if I had died with them plaguey measles I had last winter, I should have left Herb Tenney my dog, Ben Smith my sled, and some of the rest of the boys my new boots and kite, and a lots of things, but I got well.

CHIP. That's the kind of a thing that gave the stuff to the old tarnal, is it?

TOM. Yes, but then they say that Mr. Wenley made another will that give it to Viola. She has gone off to New York to be a great teacher now.

CHIP. New York, ain't that a good many miles off?

TOM. It's more than four hundred. I heard the master say so yesterday at school, but you ain't going to run away and find Viola and tell her about Betsey and what they say, are you, Chip?

CHIP. He! he! he! Guess not. Better find the will first, hadn't I, Tommy? He! he! he!

TOM. By George! I wouldn't stay here, I'll bet. Tell you what I'd do. I'd just run away in the night. Ketch me staying with that ugly old thing; I'll bet I wouldn't! But, Chip, look here, don't you tell about the will, 'cause dad 'd whip me like sixty if he knew I told of it. He tells marm that little pitchers have long ears, s'pose he means me. You won't tell, will you, Chip?

CHIP. No, not by a jug full, I won't.

BETSEY. (Outside.) Chip, you vagabond, be in here in just three minutes, I tell you. Here's all the hogs to feed and the cheese to turn in the press, and you a-lazin' out there. Stir yourself!

CHIP. (Aloud, as he and Tommy get up.) I am coming. (To himself.) When I get ready. The darned old hogs! No use feedin' 'em,—not a might; they don't grow an atom; jest stopped a-growing out o' spite, I reckon, to bother her. Nothin' would grow when she was lookin' at 'em. It's turn cheese all the time. Gosh! how I'd rip it out if I hadn't promised Viola I wouldn't. Have to hitch up my gallows or I shall bust! (Hitches up gallows.) Lazin'! First time I've stood still a minute since I've been here.

TOM. There she is now. Run, Chip, or she will be mad as a hornet.

[Exit Tommy L. 2 E. Chip starts to run, but meets Betsey, who enters R. 2 E.

BETSEY. Here, you Chip, what have you been about? I've yelled and screamed, and that's all the good it's done. For my part I wish neighbors would keep their young ones at home and not have them always hanging about other folks' houses. I'd just like to catch that saucy Tom Saunders and give him a right smart shaking up. (Shakes her fist after him and turns to Chip.) Step yourself, Chip, and do up the chores afore bed time, and see that you are up bright and early for the churning. [Betsey slaps Chip, and he runs out, she after him.

RAISE FOREST DROP SCENE.

ACT I.

Scene Third. Kitchen; Settee; Table with drawer; Chairs.

Enter Chip R. 2 E.

CHIP. I am played out, tired and sleepy as a dog. Where can I lay down so as to get out of the old tarnal's way? By jinks! I have it. (Getting under the settee.) I'll get under the settee. [Enter Betsey L. 2 E.

BETSEY. (Sitting down to table, unlocks drawer, and takes out the will and a stocking filled with silver.) Five, ten, fifteen, twenty, twenty-five. Mine! yes, all mine! Nobody to touch a dollar on't but me.

CHIP. (Sticks head out from under settee, and draws out

3

a jack-knife.) I hate her! The money is Viola's. The old tarnal stole it. I might kill her. I would take all the money and carry it to Viola. No, no, I must not kill her. Chip Winkle, Esq., the Bible Miss Viola give ye says, "Thou shalt not kill!" [Lays down.

BETSEY. Thirty, thirty-five, forty, forty-five, fifty, fifty-five. Why shouldn't I take comfort in counting it over? It is no more than right, it belongs to me. Viola come into the family and had her bringing up and schoolin', and that's what Mary Fernald's young one never ought 'a had. Amos, poor fool, to go nigh about crazy after such a hussey! He meant to leave every cent of his property and every inch of land to Viola, but, He! he! he! Betsey Smith was a little too sharp for him there. (Takes will and reads it.) This tells the story. Ha! ha! Yes, *this* tells the story. Nobody saw me, nobody knows it to this day, not a soul. (Looks about in a frightened manner.) Nobody knows it. Squire Bridgewater is dead and the witnesses are gone, and the will never had a copy; nobody knows it. I might burn it, but I won't, because I can say with a clear consciene. I never destroyed it. But I can lock it up here. (Locks will up in drawer.) And now let any one find it if they can. I'll put the money in the bank as soon as I can go to town, for I can get five per cent. on it, and laying here it don't bring in anything.

[Exit Betsey L. 2 E.

CHIP. (Getting up from under settee.) So, so, old gal, ye have given yeself away. Ye have, by vum! and I've got ye down finer than pin feathers on a hummin' bird. I'll be chawed up if I haven't. (Takes table and turns it over on the floor; pulls on drawer; takes out jack-knife, picks away at lock and finally opens it.) There, I have got it! (Opens will and reads it in a blundering manner, sitting on table) : In the name of God, Amen.

I, Amos Wenley, of Marlborough, in the county of Cheshire, and the State of New Hampshire, being weak in body. but of a sound and perfect mind and memory, (for which I have reason to praise God) do make, publish and declare this my last will and testament. and herein dispose of all my worldly estate in manner following, to wit:

First, I order and direct my executor herein named to pay all my just debts and funeral charges, soon as may be after my decease.

Second, I give and bequeath to my beloved adopted daughter, Viola May Wenley, all my property, both real and personal. May God's blessing rest upon her, and her life be a blessing and a comfort to all, as it has been to me.

Lastly, I do hereby appoint Amos A. Mason sole executor of this, my last will and testament, hereby revoking all former wills by me made.

In witness whereof I have hereunto set my hand and seal this 29th day of March in the year of our Lord [LS] one thousand eight hundred and seventy-one.

AMOS WENLEY.

Signed, sealed, published and declared by the said Amos Wenley, as and for his last will and testament, in presence of us, who at his request, in his presence and in the presence of each other, have subscribed our names as witnesses thereto.

CHARLES K. CONVERSE,
NELSON E. DAVIS,
JAMES W. COLONY.

By Jinks! that makes things all right. (Gets newspaper and does the will up in it, tying it with a long string, after which he puts it into one of his pockets and looks out at the left.) Consarn it all, I thought the old dragon had gone to the bank, but here she comes, bonnet and all. Gosh! I must hide or everything will be knocked into a smashed up hat. (Gets under settee.)

[Enter Betsey R 2 E., dressed for the street.

BETSEY. I thought I'd come back and get that money in the teapot and put with the rest. I don't need it, and robbers might steal it. I'll just slip into my bed room and get it, and then I'll be off again.

CHIP. While ye are slippin' I'll slip out. (Chip gets part way out from under settee, but hears Betsey coming and gets back again.) Didn't slip as much as I was going to.

[Enter Betsey R. 2 E.

BETSEY. (Suddenly looking out of window.) I declare if there ain't Deacon Cuff coming with his team, going to market. I'll hail him for a ride. Lucky I come back for I'll get a ride all the way now. The deacon is a-kinder hitching up to me since Amos was killed. I wouldn't have him, or any man, though. All men are plaguey fools. (Goes to door and halloos.) Deacon, deacon Cuff, I say, Deacon, stop. I want to ride.

CHIP. (Aside.) Men are such plaguey fools I shouldn't think she would ride with 'em.

DEACON. (Outside.) Whoa, whoa, Kate, whoa, whoa, will you? There, stand! Want anything, Betsey?

BETSEY. (Aside.) The old fool! I shouldn't have stopped him if I hadn't. (Hallooing to Deacon.) Yes, I want to ride. Come in and wait a minute. (To herself.) I'll make him carry some eggs and stuff to market for me, too.

[Enter Deacon at door.

DEACON. (Taking off his hat and wiping his face with red handkerchief, after which he shakes hands with Betsey.) Ah, good afternoon, Miss Betsey, you are looking as prim as a lass of sixteen. I am delighted to see you. Want to ride to the village, do you? Of course you can, with the greatest of pleasure.

BETSEY. (Aside.) Sentimental as usual. (Addressing Deacon.) Thank you, thank you, deacon. I have some eggs and things I'd like to take to market, seeing I am going right there. Is it so you can take them on your team?

DEACON. Yes, yes, without any trouble whatever. Fetch 'em along, fetch 'em along.   [Exit Betsey L. 3 E.

DEACON. A remarkable fine woman! so prudent and saving, too. Amos left her a considerable property.

CHIP. (Aside, sticking his head out.) Left it so she could steal it.

DEACON. My dear, departed Lorilla (Wipes eyes with handkerchief) has been dead over two years. (Straightening up.) Yes, I will propose to Betsey. A man of my standing, deacon of the Orthodox church, and president of the town reform club, surely needs a better-half.) Certainly I do.

CHIP. (Aside, sticking head out.) Better take half of her than the whole of her, by a darned sight.

[Enter Betsey L. 3 E., basket in hand, filled.

BETSEY. Here, Deacon, here's the produce. If you'll just take and put it on the team, I'll be right out.

DEACON. (Taking basket.) Yes, yes, Miss Betsey, yes, yes.   [Exit Deacon at door.

BETSEY. (Opening drawer.) I'll just look and see if that will is all safe, just to satisfy myself.

CHIP. (Aside, sticking his head out.) Precious safe I'd be now, if she should find me.

BETSEY. (Screams.) The will is gone. What can have become of it? Nobody has been here but Deacon Cuff. The old sinner must have stole it. What shall I do?

[Enter Deacon at door.

DEACON. (Excited.) W-h-a-t, w-h-a-t, wh-at, what's the matter?

BETSEY. I had a slight shock.

CHIP. (Aside, sticking his head out.) A will shock.

DEACON. A shock?

BETSEY. Yes, Deacon Cuff; you ain't taken anything that didn't belong to you, have you?

DEACON. (Aside.) That's a queer question to ask. (Addressing Betsey.) Nothing to do any harm.

BETSEY. What was it?

DEACON. Your basket.

BETSEY. That? I gave that to you to carry out to the wagon. I mean did you steal anything?

DEACON. (Greatly surprised.) What, me? me, Deacon Cuff, Deacon of the Orthodox church, president town reform club? me steal anything? You are crazy!

BETSEY. No, I ain't either. Some one has stole a paper that belongs to me. No one has been here but you.

DEACON. Oh, a paper! What was it? *Cheshire Republican,* or *Christian at Work?*

CHIP. (Aside, sticking head out.) No Christian's at work here. Starve to death if there was.

BETSEY. No, no, it was a legal paper!

DEACON. What kind of a legal paper?

BETSEY. A right of way through some land.

CHIP. (Aside, sticking out head.) I'll right away through the land to New York if I ever get out of here.

DEACON I have seen nothing that looks like a paper.

BETSEY. You are sure? Let me look in your pockets.

DEACON. What? What? Still think I took it when I told you I did not? I'd have you know my word is not to be doubted. (Throws himself back with dignity.) I am Deacon Cuff, deacon of the Orthodox church, and president of the town reform club, I am.

CHIP. (Aside, sticking head out.) Go it, Cuffy.

BETSEY. (Going up to him.) I don't care if you are a bishop, I am going to examine your pockets. No one has been here but you since it was here.

DEACON. (Reproachfully.) Betsey, here! I'll show you what is in my pockets. (Turns them in side out, pockets being filled with all sorts of things except papers.) There, you see I've not got anything but what belongs to me.

BETSEY. Hold on! there's an inside pocket in your coat.

DEACON. (Steps back.) T-h-e-r-e, th-e-r-e, there's nothing in it; no, nothing.

BETSEY. Let me see.

DEACON. I tell you there is nothing in it.

BETSEY. (Suddenly thrusts hand into pocket and snatches out pint whiskey bottle.) What! (Smells of it.) Why, its a whiskey—a whiskey bottle! You are a pretty man, you are, for president of a reform club.

DEACON. (In great humility.) Betsey, Betsey, you wrong me.

BETSEY. Ain't it whiskey?

DEACON. Yes, yes; but it ain't to drink.

BETSEY. Ain't to drink?

DEACON. No, no; it's to kill potato bugs. A very effective exterminator indeed.

CHIP. (Aside, sticking head out.) Kill potato bugs! Chain lightnin' wouldn't do it.

BETSEY. (Aside.) The old liar! One thing is sure enough, he's not got the will about him. Perhaps I have mislaid it; I am going to the village anyway. I must smooth things over a little. He won't say nothing, though, about my losing a legal paper, for it would give the whiskey scrape away, so that's all right. (Addressing Deacon and giving him back the bottle.) Here, deacon, here's your bottle; I should judge whiskey would kill 'em; I'm glad you told me. I guess, after all, deacon, I didn't lose anything; the shock unstrung my nerves. Excuse my actions, will you?

DEACON. Certainly, certainly, but, I say, don't say anything about the potato bug exterminator. You know folks would talk if they knew I put liquor to any use.

BETSEY. Of course I won't say anything. As you say, folks are liable to talk if there is any ground whatever, especially about men so prominent as yourself. Are you ready to go to town now? I am.

DEACON. Yes, yes; I was so flustered I forgot to ask if you were ready. Will you take my arm?

[Exit Deacon and Betsey at door, arm in arm.

CHIP. (Getting out from under settee.) Gosh! what a go. Whiskey and potato bugs. Ha, ha, ha! Now is my time to skip. I'll do it, too.

[Exit at L. 2 E., returning with bundle done up in a red handkerchief, slung over his back on a stick.

CHIP. Chip Winkle, Esq., is bound for New York with "The Stolen Will." Good bye until Viola is found.

FRONT CURTAIN.

ACT II.

Scene First. Parlor. Madam Loker and Sarah Loker sitting by table. Center Table. Three Chairs.

MADAM. (Fanning.) Sadie, you have, without doubt, noticed that Mr. Jameson has been quite attentive to me since your father died. Well, last evening he proposed, and he being rich and accomplished, I accepted. Now, my dear, your cousin Edward is coming home from Europe, soon, and all you have to do is to lay your ropes and follow your mamma's example. We will be married at the same time if it can be arranged.

SARAH. (Languidly fanning.) You do not mean to say

you are engaged, do you? 'T is grand! May I have as good success with Edward.' His first wife's child, Cora, is the only stumbling block.

MADAM. Nay, not a stumbling block, but a help. Sadie, you must win him through Cora, for he worships her, and by making of the child, you can win him, as you otherwise never could.

SARAH. But I hate children. It's bad enough to marry a widower, without a child. No offense to you, mamma. He's rich and refined; that's one consolation.

FOOTMAN. (Outside.) Well, miss, what do you want?

VIOLA. (Outside.) I am expected.

FOOTMAN. (Outside.) You be, be you. Well, I should think so, by the looks.

VIOLA. (Outside.) Go to your mistress instantly; tell her that Miss Wenley is here.

[Madam arises and goes to door.

MADAM. John is getting pompous. (In a high key.) It's the new governess, John; show her up.

[Enter footman at door, followed by Viola. Exit footman at door.

MADAM. (Sitting down.) Ah, you have come, then, for I presume I address the young lady recommended by Madam Spofford. Take a seat.

VIOLA. (Taking a seat.) Thanks. I was sent by Madam Spofford.

MADAM. Miss Wenley, I had no doubt but Madam Spofford would send an older person; you look very young. The last governess was much older.

VIOLA. I am young; not quite eighteen, but I shall be growing older every day.

MADAM. Ah, yes, but that is very young. Oh, excuse me! Sadie, this is the new teacher. (Sarah just glances up from a novel she is reading.) You are quite tall, Miss Wenley, but too slender. Are you strong, miss?

VIOLA. (Arising.) Madam, is my size, or strength, or years the criterion of my qualifications to teach your children? Madam Spofford's statement involved my scholarship, I believe.

MADAM. Dear me! Why, Miss Wenley, you are too hasty. I meant nothing of the kind, I assure you. Pray sit down. (Viola sits down.) Your youth seems objectionable only so far as your power of governing is concerned. And yet, after all, it may be best, for you will enter more into the feelings of the children. They always complained that Miss Stone was too stiff and unbending. You see, my dear, (smiles condescendingly,) I, for one, don't believe in taxing teachers too hard, nor pupils, either. Thus, you see, your duties will not be hard, no dull, flagging scholars to urge along, for Marky is uncommonly clever; indeed, Dr. Merriam assures me that Marky, though somewhat peculiar, is prematurely developed in all his mental faculties; and Cora, little Cora Enwright, my nephew's child, whose home is with us, is quite a good scholar. Marky's passion for music is really wonderful. You are an accomplished player, Madam Spofford writes me. Do you sing also?

VIOLA. Yes, Madam.

MADAM. Well, I am glad of that, for Miss Stone had no voice; Marky will be delighted, as will Cora. As regards management, you will find the children perfectly submissive. Perhaps now and then a little exuberance of spirits on Marky's part will need restraint, but usually he is an affectionate and yielding child.

VIOLA. I am very fond of children.

MADAM. Well, they will be but very little trouble. (Noise outside.) There is Marky, now. Rather noisy, I declare. That Kathleen! dear me, me! I must dismiss her. She does not manage right with Marky; always crossing him.

MARKY. (Outside, crying and kicking.) I won't; no, I won't; let me alone. I won't, I tell you.

KATHLEEN. (Outside.) Marky Loker, you be still. Be still, I tell you.

MARKY. (Outside.) I won't, I won't; no, I won't.

SARAH. (Puts hands over ears.) Dear me, mamma, how shocking!

MADAM. (Arising and going to door.) I've no doubt but what Kathleen has been crossing him in some harmless sport. These Irish girls are so impatient. It seems her special delight to worry my darling. (In a high key.) Kathleen, fetch Marky in.

[Enter Kathleen L. 3 E., followed by Marky.

MADAM. What's this noise all about?

MARKY. (Crying.) Kate won't rock me. She said I was too big to be rocked.

KATHLEEN. That he is, madam!

MARKY. No, I ain't either. Ma, make her rock me, do!

VIOLA. Madam, if you please, I will be shown to my room.

MADAM. Ah, bless me! I had forgotten you might be weary. You came by the boat, I presume, and they are dreadful for making one sick, especially when the Sound is rough. In consideration of your journey, you need not commence your duties in the school-room until tomorrow. Kathleen, take Marky away and then return and show Miss Wenley to her room.

KATHLEEN. (Bowing.) Yes, madam.

MARKY. (Crying.) I won't go a step, unless Kate carries me; So I won't. I am tired.

KATHLEEN. (Taking Marky by arm.) Come along with me. [Exit Kathleen L. 3 E., with Marky.

MADAM. Be careful with him, Kathleen. (Turning to Viola.) We shall be obliged to put you in the sky loft chamber for a short time. Sadie is to give a birthday party next week, and all the rooms down stairs will be taken. After that we will give you a better room.

VIOLA. (Aside.) And this is the place to wnich I have been looking forward to, as a happy, refined home. This is what I have educated myself for—to teach wild, spoiled, romping children,—to be little better than a hired nursery girl. What a trial it will be! That purse proud, vulgar woman, that haughty daughter with her doll face and insolent stare. Better far to go forth and do anything,—teach the children of the backwoods; do anything that is honorable. [Enter Kathleen L. 3 E.

KATHLEEN. Now I am after showing you to your room, if you are ready, miss.

VIOLA. Thanks.

[Exit Kathleen R. 3 E., followed by Viola. Enter Footman at door followed by Jameson.

FOOTMAN. (Bows.) Mr. George Jameson.

[Exit Footman at door.

JAMESON. (Bowing to Madam and Sarah who return bow.) Ah. how do you do, Florence, my love? I am delighted to see you, Miss Sadie.

[Exit Sarah L. 2 E.

MADAM. Be seated, please. (Jameson sits down.) How kind of you, George, to call; I was dying to see you. Sadie is delighted over our engagement.

JAMESON. I am so glad. (Aside.) It will be easier managing the old woman's property. She thinks I am rich; so I am, in a horn. (Addressing Madam.) Who was that young lady that went out of here as I came in?

MADAM. The new governess, Miss Wenley.

JAMESON. (Aside.) Viola, as sure as fate! But it makes no odds; she does not know who I am. (Addressing Madam.) Oh!

MADAM. Seeing you are soon to become a member of the family,—to be a father to Marky,—I should be pleased to

4

have you present to-morrow when the governess drills him and Edward's child, to see what studies they are adapted to.

JAMESON. (Aside.) I'd pursue a course taking that fool of a Marky to an idiot asylum. (Addressing Madam.) Thanks, I should be delighted to be present. Marky is a fine boy and I already love him as though he was of my own flesh and blood.

MADAM. (Murmurs.) Oh, George, how kind-hearted you are. How happy we shall be when we are married.

JAMESON. (Aside.) I'll be happy to get her money, that's all. (Addressing Madam.) Yes, our hearts will beat as one.
[Noise outside. Enter Marky L. 3 E.

MARKY. (Crying.) Kathleen won't play horse with me.

MADAM. That girl shall be discharged! Marky, cheer up and come here. Mr. Jameson wants to see you. (Marky stops crying; walks up with finger in his mouth.) Marky, Mr. Jameson is going to be your father. Kiss him, Marky.

MARKY. (Failing to kiss Jameson.) I don't want to. I've had one father; ain't that enough?

MADAM. But, Marky, he is to be your step-father, and will love you as though you were his own boy. Come, now, kiss him.

MARKY. What! love me the same as father used to Kate, when you wan't around? He used to kiss her; must I love him like that?

MADAM. (Aside.) I'll turn that girl off at once. Addressing Marky.) Your father never kissed Kathleen. Come, kiss Mr. Jameson. (Marky does so.) That's right.

JAMESON. (Aside.) Bah! I never thought I should kiss such a calf. (Addressing Madam.) A very nice boy!

MADAM. Yes, and so clever! Why, he speaks French like a native. Will you try him in the language?

JAMESON. If you wish. (Madam inclines head.) *Parles vous Francais.*

MARKY. *Oui.*

JAMESON. *Bon jour.*

MARKY. *Oui.*

JAMESON. (Smiling.) *Bon soir.*

MARKY. *Oui.*

JAMESON. *N'aubliez pas.*

MARKY. *Oui.*

JAMESON. I am afraid you are a little mixed in your French to-day.

MADAM. Yes, I am surprised, but it is not your fault, Marky. Miss Stone did not teach you as she should. The first question you answered correctly, but the rest wrong.

Bon jour is "good morning" and you should have repeated it, as you should *Bon soir*, which is "good evening." The last phrase was "forget not," and you should have answered in the negative. Now, Marky, run and play.

[Exit Marky L. 3 E. Enter Footman L. 2 E.

FOOTMAN. Miss Sadie has ordered the carriage and is going down to the park. She wishes to know if you will accompany her.

MADAM. Is it so you can go, George?

JAMESON. Certainly.

MADAM. We will go at once.

[Exit Footman L. 2 E. followed by Jameson and Madam arm in arm.

RAISE PARLOR CURTAIN.

ACT II.

Scene Second. Schoolroom. Five Chairs, Table, Organ, Globe, Maps and Books. Madam Loker, Sarah Loker, George Jameson seated at left, Marky and Cora Enwright seated at right. [Enter Viola L. 2 E.

MADAM. Ah, good morning. We were waiting for you. Mr. Jameson, Miss Wenley, Miss Wenley, Mr. Jameson. (Jameson and Viola bow.) This gentleman is about to become a member of the family, and is, of course, interested in the children, especially Marky.

JAMESON. (Aside.) To think she is a governess.

VIOLA. (Aside.) The same dark complected man that followed me when at school. What can it mean? (Addressing Madam and nodding towards the children.) These are my pupils, I suppose.

MADAM. Yes, children, this is your new teacher, Miss Wenley. Marky, let Miss Wenley hear you recite in geography. Name the New England states.

MARKY. (In a loud voice, and opening and shutting a large jack-knife.) Maine, Vermont, Massachusetts, Rhode Island, New Hampshire and Connecticut.

MADAM. Bound New York.

MARKY. New York is bounded on the North by Lake Ontario and St. Lawrence river, on the east by Vermont, on the south by Pennsylvania and on the west by Sing Sing.

MADAM. Be careful, Marky; It's bounded on the west by Lak e Erie and Pennsylvania. What's the capital?

MARKY. Buffalo.

MADAM. You are not up in your geography to-day; Albany is the capital.

MARKY. Albany is the capital.

MADAM. Who's the President of the United States. and who is Governor of New York?

MARKY. James G. Blaine, President United States ; Henry Ward Beecher, Governor New York. (Cuts his finger and runs to Madam to be consoled. She ties handkerchief around it.)

MADAM. There, there, Marky, don't cry ; Miss Wenley wants to ask you some questions.

VIOLA. Now, Marky, let's hear you repeat the multiplication table.

SARAH. (Aside.) Wonder if she would not like to have the days of the week repeated.

MARKY. (Stops crying, says the one's part through, every now and then looking to Viola to see if he is right.) There. Mamma. it's no use ! I am stuck. Didn't I tell you that Will Putney. if he is the cook's boy and lives in the kitchen, can beat me in 'rithmetic. (Turns to Viola.) I can't say it, Ma'am, I never went to school with the other boys. Will, he knows it by heart. (Opens and shuts knife and cries.)

MADAM. No matter, my son ; don't cry. Go now to your seat, but do put up that horrid knife ; I am fearful you will hurt yourself. (Marky sits down ; Madam turns to Viola.) You see, Miss Wenley, I never approved of putting children into the city schools where they come in contact with everybody's. Marky was always delicate, and I particularly requested the last teacher not to tax him. Dr. Merriam assures me I ought not, and that will account for his seeming deficiency in some of the elementary studies. Now, when he takes to a study, one might as well endeavor to move the battery as turn him from it. The doctor says " never cramp or distort a young mind." and I have always allowed Marky his own bent. (Speaking to Cora) Cora, let Miss Wenley hear you recite some piece. [Cora arises, bows and speaks :

"I WONDER!"

"I look at the sky and wonder.
O starry deeps! What is the mystery
That hurls your orbs in perfect, sweet accord?
Oft times obscured by fleecy ships of cloud ;
Again grown pale in Luna's matchless smile.
Why are ye not precipitated down?
And in a vast chaotic whirlpool thrown
To dance, and seethe, and bubble into nought?
Ye gemmy isles that star celestial seas,
Say : art thou gleaners in the fields of space?
Art blossoms hung is spring's prelatent crown?
Art precious sands strewn on the shores of time?
Tell me : What art thou? And why art thou there?
When lurid lightnings lick the vaulted sky,
Are ye not pierced by wrathful javelines thrown?
And strung like golden beads upon a thread?
Fit necklace to enring the tempest's throat.

Or is the purple ocean where ye bathe
And prattle at reflections of yourselves
So far and vast ye do not even know
Of storms that vex the bosom of our star?
Reveal to me the law which governs you;
The one intelligence which guides you all.
For sure but one intelligence above
Could tune you to such perfect harmony.
And to my spirit's questioning, there comes
But one sweet answer: GOD!

"I look in my soul and wonder:
O soul! thou fiery chariot of thought!
Thou fountain of the affections! Thou throne
Of all infinite possibilities!
Vaster in thy compass than the stars;
Deeper than the ocean of the skies;
Richer, in being soul, than all the wealth
That treasured in Phœbus coffers lie:
And dearer to the heart of Infinite,
Than universe, suns and moons and stars.
Where gathered, and what are the elements
That form thee? O, thou strange mysterious soul!
Or art thou some new element thyself?
Or that which animates an element?
Didst preexist ere by the body caught,
And prisoned in its tenement of dust?
Art thou like plants, that grow, and leaf and bloom,
In slow unfoldment? Or art perfect formed?
And openest the treasures of thy store
But as the growth of spirit may demand?
If this, O burst the shroud that veileth thee,
And let my eager spirit drink, O soul!
From thy full fountain, quenchingly and deep.
I pray you, tell me: part of what art thou?
Still to my spirit's questioning, there comes
The same sweet answer: GOD!"

[All look pleased with piece.

VIOLA. (Kissing Cora.) Excellent! A difficult piece for a person of mature years to speak. Where did you learn it?

CORA. Papa wrote it, and I learned it, so to speak it when he comes home. He is the best of good men, Miss Wenley.

[Cora resumes seat.

VIOLA. He must be if his child resembles him.

MADAM. Don't flatter the child, please. (Aside.) Edward might fall in love with the governess if the child should take to her.

SARAH. Cora, dear, come and stand by me. (Cora does so; Sarah puts arm around her and kisses her, saying aside) I suppose I have got to make of her if I hope to win her father.

MARKY. I want to speak a piece. Cora don't know any more than I do; no, she don't.

[Strikes an attitude and speaks:

Here I stand upon the stage!
Oh, don't I cut a figure?
If you do not like my piece
Just wait till I get bigger.

MADAM. Marky, that will do.

SARAH. You are a fool, Mark Loker.

JAMESON. (Aside.) I agree with the daughter.

[Viola suppresses laughter. Cora looks surprised.

MADAM. Miss Wenley, will you please play and sing? I desire that the children shall be thoroughly instructed in music.

[Viola sits down to organ and plays and sings some popular piece.

MADAM. Ah, pretty—very pretty. I dare say you are an accomplised organist ; Madam Spofford recommended you as such, but Monsieur Figaro would say you lacked style. Now my Sadie,—she will play for you some day in the drawing-room ; her organ is superb, quite different from this the children practice on ; my nephew, Cora's father, the Hon. Edward Enwright, selected it in London. Sadie was at a boarding school then. Well, as I was saying, Monsieur pronounces her style *brilliante magnifique*. But really ! (Draws gold watch from pocket and consults it.) Almost ten ! (Turns to Jameson and Sarah) and we have an engagement at eleven. We must be going. (Exit Jameson, Sarah, and Madam L. 2 E., arm in arm, Madam continuing). Your dinner will be served in the nursery with the children. Good morning !

VIOLA. Good morning !

STREET DROP SCENE.

ACT II.

Scene Third. Street. Signs on buildings, among others, being " Wright & Co.," " Hardy & Co.," Brown & Co."

[Enter Chip, R. 2 E.

CHIP. By vum ! Here I am in the town of New York. (Looking up at signs.) Well, I be goll darned if here ain't still another sign with Mr. Co.'s name on it. I'd just like to know who this Mr. Co. is ; he seems to own about everything 'round here. (Reads signs.) " Wright & Co.," " Hardy & Co.," " Brown & Co." As Granny White used to sing " still there 's more to follow," for all I know. Everybody seems to be in company with Co., I'll be blest if they don't. By jingo ! New York is a mighty big town, bigger than all git out ; monstrous high stone walls ; folks call 'em houses ; folks are fearful queer, I'll be shot if they ain't ; ask 'em where Miss Viola lives, they laugh and don't know a darned thing.

Bet if there was gal right over there, (Points) and ye ask 'em who 's that gal over there? they wouldn't know a plaguey thing, but jest laugh ; reg'lar set of fools, anyhow. (Draws the will from his pocket, looks at it and returns it.) He, he, he ! think I am a fool, do they? Perhaps I be, but I'll bet Betsey Smith don't think so. Chip Winkle, Esq., knows a thing or two. He, he, he ! I'd give my black and white rabbit and pet rooster I've got up in New Hampshire, and everything else I've got, too, to find Miss Viola. Yes, siree! I'd do it! (Looking out at left.) Gracious! here comes a blue thing; it's a-fire! Fire! fire! fire!

[Enter in haste Cop, L. 2 E., cigar in mouth.

Cop. Fire! Where? Where? Speak up.

Chip. (Surprised.) Fire? Where? Why, ye darned fool, ye are a-fire yourself! (Aside.) He's crazy. I can't get him out alone. (Yells) Fire! Fire!

Cop. (Grabbing Chip by arm and shaking him.) You young rascal, what do you mean? I ain't a-fire!

Chip. Yes, you be, too. That thing in your mouth is red hot, and smoke is pouring right of you.

Cop. That's nothing. I am only smoking a cigar. (Aside.) Lucky for me no one else caught me smoking on the beat, or I would be reported.

Chip. A what?

Cop. A cigar.

Chip. What's that?

Cop. Why, you fool, it is tobacco rolled up to smoke. Didn't you ever see any one smoke before?

Chip. My name ain't " You Fool"; it's Chip Winkle, Esq.

Cop. Oh! it is, is it?

Chip. Yes. I've seen folks have things made to smoke —pipes. I never see a stick or what ye call a cigar all a-fire before. Don't get mad; I thought ye was a-fire, I did. Do all ye blue things—ye fellers with brass coats trimmed with blue buttons—smoke these things?

Cop. Well, well, I declare! You are a queer coon. Blue things! Why, blue things! they are policemen. I am one.

Chip. Oh, a circus feller!

Cop. No, no, a policeman is an officer of the law, who is 'round when there's a row, and arrests folks for breaking the law.

Chip. I know, now. There was a fight up-street, here, while ago, and I see one after the row was through. Policemen have to get 'round as soon as a row is through, don't they? Some one yelled out " There's a rainbow," and another feller hallooed back, " There's always a rainbow after a storm." The policeman he looked mad, shook a stick at 'em; heard 'em say it was a billy, but it didn't look a might like any Bill I ever knew. They yelled away at the policeman, and he kept a-getting mad and madder. At last he grabs a little bit of a youngster and started off with him; they said for the station house. I didn't hear said what railroad

it was station for. Some one said something about Black
Maria; I kinder thought it might be that she or some of her
folks was connected with the road; she must be a big lady
about here, for I have heard lots of folks tell on her.

Cop. (Laughing long and hearty.) Well, well, this beats
all I ever heard of. (Laughing.) A station house is where
they lock folks up, and the Black Maria is a team for transporting prisoners.

Chip. I've transplanted cabbages and the like; never
heard of transplanting folks before. Do they grow well?

Cop. Transporting is what I said, not transplanting. But
come, my lad, you must be moving. And look a' here, don't
you halloo on the street again; you will find yourself in a
station house if you do, and stand a chance of getting ac-
quainted with the Black Maria.

Chip. Feller can't do nothin' in New York.

[Exit Chip L. 2 E.

Cop. Barnum ought to have this Chip Winkle, Esq.

[Exit Cop, R. 2 E. Enter Viola L. 2 E., leading Cora,
followed by Marky wheeling a child's wheelbarrow with a rag
baby in it.

Viola. We must hurry home; it's getting late, and we
have been gone quite a while.

Marky. (Cries.) I don't want to go home. No, I don't.

Cora. But, Marky, we must, for, as Viola says, it's getting late.

Marky. That's it; you always agree with what she says.
I won't go home; no, I won't.

Viola. (Aside to Cora.) Come, Cora, we will go, and
he will follow fast enough, for he will be afraid of getting lost.
(To Marky.) We are going, and you had better come.

[Exit Viola and Cora R. 2 E.

(Marky wheels barrow back and forth, smiling and happy as
you please. All at once he drops wheelbarrow and begins
to cry.) [Enter Police, L. 2 E.

Police. (Walks past, and suddenly looks up; sees Marky
and turns round to him. Looks at him and gets ladder at
wings at right; puts up against him and climbs up and pats
him on the head.) What's the matter with you, my little
man?

Marky. (Crying.) I'm lost.

Police. You are? Who are you?

Marky. (Crying.) I'm mother's fair-haired, darling little boy.

Police. What's your mother's name, and where do you
live?

MARKY. (Crying.) Same as mine—Loker. Live up on Fifth Avenue.

POLICE. (Getting down and putting ladder up side of building again.) Well, come with me, my little man, and I'll take you to your mother.

[Exit Police. leading Marky, who drags wheelbarrow by one handle, and clings to rag baby, R. 2 E.

[Enter Chip on the run, L. 2 E.

CHIP. I see Miss Viola go by with a little gal, and something else. Queer looking object, anyway. Now I've got track of her, I'll find her. Then Betsey Smith, ye want to look out. [Exit Chip R. 2 E.

RAISE STREET DROP SCENE.

ACT II.

Scene Fourth. Parlor. Centre Table, three Chairs. Madam Loker and Sarah Loker seated.

MADAM. Sadie, it is perfectly unaccountable,—the fancy Edward's child takes to this governess. This morning I was forced to send her away she clung to her so ; and just now. passing the school room, I saw her through the half open door, in her lap, and the governess hugging and kissing her as though she had found a treasure. But I sent Kathleen up instantly after the child. Artful creature, I'll warrant she is ; these poor teachers always are. You don't suppose, Sadie, this fondling round the child is for the sake of her father? She is handsome,—he might take a fancy to her ; I have a good mind to send her away.

SARAH. (Laughing.) Nonsense, mamma, how perfectly ridiculous ! Cousin Edward is in Europe, and this poor country governess never dreamed of him. Bah ! What strange ideas run in your head.

MADAM. You must remember that she saved Cora from being run over at the risk of her own life. That will give her a strong claim on his affections, and affection begets love, and love, marriage. If I am over anxious, Sadie, remember it is for your sake ; you know on what I have set my heart when Edward returns.

SARAH. Your heart is set on that no more than mine, mamma ; I have not slighted so many hearts to go unrewarded. Edward Enwright shall be mine.

[Noise outside. Enter Footman at door, followed by Enwright.

FOOTMAN. (Bows.) The Hon. Edward Enwright.

[Exit Footman at door.

(Madam and Sarah both rise at once.)

5

ENWRIGHT. Ah, aunt! cousin! I am delighted.

MADAM. (Shaking hands.) A pleasant surprise.

SARAH. (Shaking hands.) Welcome home from a foreign shore. [All three sit down.

MADAM. When did you come? We had seen no announcement of the arrival of the steamer.

ENWRIGHT. We made port about an hour ago, and I hurried here at once, anxious to see you and Cora. Where is she?

SARAH. With Kathleen, Edward.

MADAM. Sadie and Kathleen rival one another in seeing who shall have the care of Cora.

ENWRIGHT. It gives me pleasure to hear that my darling has so devoted attendants. Please send for her.

[Madam rings for Footman. Footman enters L. 2 E. and bows.

MADAM. Bring Cora here, John.

[Footman bows, and exits L. 2 E.

MADAM. You see I have made no change in my establishment since poor Mr. Loker died. Not that I cared to continue here, my dear nephew; Oh, no, no, some more retired home would have accorded far better with a poor, bereaved woman's feeling, but I thought of Sadie, how dull it would be after her graduation, and for her sake remained here. When I opened the house for her coming out party it seemed like opening a tomb; but I struggled hard with such feelings; society has claims on us all, you know, (Glances at Sarah) especially the young.

SARAH. (Aside.) She knows he will think it strange of us, keeping up such appearances on our income, and is excusing it. Mamma is so clever. (Addressing Enwright.) Ah, here comes Cora, darling.

[Enter, Footman, with Cora, L 2 E. Footman bows to Madam, exits L. 2 E.

CORA. (Runs to Enwright and kisses him.) Oh, papa, I am so glad you have come.

ENWRIGHT. No more than I am to come. How does my little girl do?

CORA. Nicely; I have got one of the best of governesses who takes the best of care of me. Why, one day I got in the way of a team, as we were out walking, and she saved me at the risk of her own life, so those that saw it said. You will be sure and like her, papa.

ENWRIGHT. What is this I hear, aunt, about Cora being rescued by a governess?

MADAM. Oh, she was out walking with the governess, and

through carelessness on the part of the governess, came near being hurt.

SARAH. That's all!

CORA. She was n't careless. It was all Marky's fault, for he pushed me in front of a team. She pulled me away.

MADAM. Cora has got a mistaken idea. (Aside.) The governess shall be discharged.

SARAH. Yes, a mistaken idea.

MADAM. How did you enjoy yourself in Europe?

ENWRIGHT. Travel wearies; foreign lands cease to charm. The old world with its classical antiquities, the treasures of art, ruins and temples, fallen obelisks and eternal pyramids, ancient libraries and galleries of painting and sculpture, Italian sunsets and glacial Alps, pall on the taste after a season, and the wanderer's eye turns longingly homeward over the ocean. The simplest thing—a voice, a strain of music—has power to bring the homesick tear to the eye. I can understand now why the Marsellaise so stirs anew all the old fires of bravery in the enthusiastic Frenchman's breast; why the Swiss peasant so yearns for his native mountains when Alpine songs are sung, and why the sound of the bag-pipe brings the Highland lochs and glens and the heather bells to the memory of Scotia's wandering sons. One day,—it was in Florence, and I had just left a picture gallery where I had lounged away a half day and was passing an old cathedral, when I heard a familiar strain that made my heart leap for joy; and what do you think it was?

SARAH. The *Casta Diva*, or *Il Trovatore*, sung in their own liquid Italian, or any opera you may have heard prima donnas warble at your theatres, and which salute your ear at every turn in Italian cities. I would wager a box of gloves I am right.

ENWRIGHT. You would lose. There stood, in front of the cathedral steps, a poor, half-clad beggar boy, strumming the strings of an old guitar to the stirring accompaniment of Yankee Doodle.

MADAM AND SARAH. Yankee Doodle!

ENWRIGHT. Yes, Yankee Doodle. Now I am not naturally enthusiastic or over patriotic, but, I declare, that thrilled me like a trumpet call—the trumpet call of freedom. There in down-trodden, priest-ridden, enslaved Italy, the very street beggars sung the stirring national song of a great and glorious republic. Does it not prove, I argued, that no thrall, no enslavement, can utterly crush out the inborn yearning for freedom which the Creator has implanted in every human heart. And straightway I had builded a most fair and powerful structure—a very temple of liberty with domes and towering spires rending the blue Florence sky—and all these reared on the flimsiest of foundations,—an Italian beggar's broken version of our national hymn. And when, at the close, those sad, dreamy eyes looks wishfully into mine and an outstretched olive-hued hand was presented to me, and the boy implored, in bad English, charity of the Signor, half the contents of my purse was enthusiastically awarded him. I was not giving alms to a lazy beggar, oh, no ; I was investing a few coins of " filthy lucre " toward the embodiment of a noble principle—liberty. But, alas, for my delightful air castles ! Wandering that way again, half an hour later, what do you think greeted me?

MADAM. I am sure I cannot tell.

SARAH. And I should fare as badly in guessing as I did before.

ENWRIGHT. The refrain of an air strangely like "God save the King" died away, and I came suddenly upon my youthful hero, clad in a gay scarlet tunic, lazily sunning himself on the steps of the church *Santa Crace*, alternately humming the above named monarchical song and greedily devouring that favorite of Italian beggars—maccaroni—which, together with the gay tunic, were the very democratic investments of my charity. Ha, ha, that was the end of my enthusiasm. Down, down, like a plummet dropped into the Adriatic, sunk my temple of liberty,—spires, domes, national emblems and all. The dreamy-eyed Italian beggar boy was speedily transformed into a roguish, lazy specimen of the " great unwashed," and the comparison I involuntarily made between the sons of our sturdy Anglo Saxon race and the enslaved children of the effeminate Southland, was anything but inspiring. American soldiers starving at Valley Forge, and dirty Italian beggars ; Yankee Doodle and maccaroni ! Bah ! I went to my hotel a sadder and wiser man. But this is a digression ; I wished to tell you that the Italian beggar boy's song answered one purpose—perhaps not an unimportant one, since it sent me home. Yes, it set me to thinking. A breath of air from my country home at Springdale seemed to sweep over me. The first Mediterranean vessel bore me as a passenger. So had my cosmopolitan tastes grown upon me that I came near forgetting the child I had left behind, a care to others. I came home at once.

SARAH. No, cousin Edward ; no, you wrong us. Cora has been no care ; on the contrary, the light and joy of the house. For her sake, no less than yours, is she dear to us.

MADAM. Yes, indeed, nephew. I love the child the same as my own darling.

ENWRIGHT. Thank you, thank you, both my dear aunt and cousin. This is very grateful to me. Yet, do not think for the three long years the world has claimed me, I have ceased to remember what drove me there,—the death of my dear wife. The old wound rankles yet. Come, Cora, let's take a walk. *Au revoir.*

MADAM AND SARAH. *Au revoir.*

[Exit Enwright and Cora L. 2 E.

MADAM. Sadie, my dear, Edward is somewhat changed. He will never forget his life with Carrie, or her death. I believe he is one of the kind who never forget. Do you think he will ever marry again?

SARAH. Beauty will never win him ; much as he may admire he never would marry again for it. Mamma, there is but one avenue to his proud heart ; whoever would win Edward Enwright, it is plain, must love his child—must play the tender, domestic, humdrum woman. I wonder if I am equal to that. (Gets up and views herself in glass and scornfully remarks) I am your very humble, devoted servant, cousin mine, until I win you.

MADAM. You must win him. (Looks at watch.) It is time to dress for dinner.

[Exit Madam and Sarah. L. 2 E. Enter Enwright, hat and cane in hand, and Cora, R. 2 E.

CORA. How nice it seems, papa, to have you at home.

[Enwright and Cora sit down.

ENWRIGHT. Yes, home is the place of all places. Payne truly says, " Be it ever so humble, there's no place like home, sweet home." How sad to think he never had a home and died in a foreign land. Cora, always have pity for the homeless.

CORA. I do, papa. The governess, Miss Wenley, has no home ; her papa and mamma are both dead. She is so good and nice I love her awful well.

ENWRIGHT. Hearing you speak of her, Cora, has really interested me in her. I should be pleased to meet the lady.

CORA. You cannot help liking her.

[Enter Viola L. 2 E.

VIOLA. (Stepping back.) Excuse me for intruding. I was lonesome and was looking for Cora, not knowing friends were present with her. (Turns to leave.) I will retire.

ENWRIGHT. Do not leave on my account, I pray. I presume you are the governess.

VIOLA. Yes, sir.

ENWRIGHT. I am Cora's father. Pray be seated.

CORA. Yes, do sit down. I want you and papa to like one another. [Enwright and Viola laugh. Viola sits down.

CORA. Well, I do.

ENWRIGHT. Cora says you saved her from being run over. Accept my thanks and rest assured mere thanks will not be all.

VIOLA. Don't mention it; I only did my duty.

[Enter Footman L. 2 E.

FOOTMAN. (Bowing to Enwright.) Madam wishes to see you in the library at once.

ENWRIGHT. (Arising.) I will go immediately. Cora, you can stay with Miss Wenley. (Aside.) This governess is just the one I should prefer to marry. Cora likes her, and she is handsome and accomplished. (Kissing Cora.) Good bye, pet. (Bowing to Viola.) Good day.

[Exit Enwright and Footman L. 2 E. Enter Marky L. 1 E.

MARKY. Ma says she ain't going to have you and Cora's pa making love; she knew you were in here, and sent for him.

VIOLA. The idea! (Aside.) He's a splendid man.

CORA. They were n't making love; they were only talking.

VIOLA. Come, children, it is time to recite your lessons.

[Exit Viola, leading Cora and Marky, R. 2 E. Enter Footman, followed by Jameson, at door.

FOOTMAN. Be seated, sir. The ladies will be down presently. [Exit Footman at door. Jameson takes seat.

JAMESON. So this young widower, Edward Enwright, has returned from Europe. Well, well, between mamma and daughter, he will be caught in the matrimonial net, no doubt. By jove! these women beat the Dutch. Why, until to-day I supposed that Madam was wealthy, but I find that she is not. Bless my eyes, if she has not accepted me, thinking I was wealthy; yes, for money. Well, it is a case of diamond cut diamond, that's all. This is my last visit here, and then for fields anew. [Enter Chip at door.

JAMESON. (Arising and speaking aside.) Amos Wenley's bound boy, as sure as fate. What in the name of wonder can he want, and how did he get here? It won't do to let him know I know him. It might make things unpleasant concerning old Wenley's murder. (Addressing Chip.) Who are you, and where did you come from? Come, speak up.

CHIP. Chip,—Chip Winkle, Esq., from Wenley farm.

JAMESON. Laughingly, aside.) Might send for Madam and have the Squire marry us. (Addressing Chip.) Well, where is Wenley farm?

CHIP. Up to Marlborough, New Hampshire, on the bank of the Minniewawar river.

JAMESON. Oh, I know; it's on the line of the Manchester and Keene railroad.

CHIP. A man chased her in Keene on the railroad! What are ye talking about?

JAMESON. You didn't catch my meaning. I said that Marlborough was on the Manchester and Keene railroad.

CHIP. Ketch! I didn't know you throwed anything. Marlborough on a railroad? Why, darn it all! don't ye know any more than to suppose any one would build on a railroad? They'd git run over.

JAMESON. You don't understand! There is a railroad running through Marlborough that is called the Manchester and Keene railroad, and when a railroad goes through a place they call the place on the line of the road.

CHIP. Oh, ye don't say! Well, there is something that goes through the place they call a railroad. It is so far out of the town it don't amount to anything; guess it is called the Manchester and Keene. I never knew of its running, though. I thought it laid still where it was built, so cars could be run over it.

JAMESON. That's what we mean by a road running—cars going over it.

CHIP. Oh!

JAMESON. Well, what sent you here?

CHIP. Come to find Miss Viola; she lives here, for I saw her come in. The door was open and I walked in. Thought sne was in here, but she ain't; I must find her,—where is she?

JAMESON. Oh, you mean the governess: a tall, dark complected girl, with black hair and eyes.

CHIP. Yes, that's Miss Viola, but I didn't know she had married a governor.

JAMESON. (Laughing.) A governess is what we call a teacher.

CHIP. Oh!

JAMESON. (Aside.) I must find out what he wants of the girl; perhaps there is money in it. (Addressing Chip.) What do you want of her, my lad? Come, tell me, I am the lady's friend and it's all right.

CHIP. Are ye?

JAMESON. Yes.

CHIP. Well, you see, after Viola left New Hampshire to come to New York, I heard folks thought there was another will, giving the property Betsey Smith had got from Mr. Wenley, to Viola. You know Mr. Wenley was murdered, and when they settled things up, they found all the stuff was left to the housekeeper, Betsey Smith, and Miss Viola, his adopted gal, was left without a cent. The old tarnal turned her out doors.

JAMESON. Well, what's all this got to do with your being here?

CHIP. Hold on, and I'll tell ye.

JAMESON. Fire away, but cut it short.

CHIP. Well, give a feller a chance, won't ye? Folks said they thought there was another will giving the stuff to Miss Viola ; I found the will folks thought there should be, and here it is. (Takes will from pocket done up in a newspaper, tied with a lot of twine, unties it and gives it to Jameson.) I cuts and runs away when I finds it. Old Betsey Smith is mad, I bet.

JAMESON. (Reading will, speaks aside.) I see a chance to make a stake, but I must bluff the boy off. (Addressing Chip.) This is a will, as you say, and it gives Wenley Farm and the Wenley money to Viola May Wenley, the governess. Boy, it is not safe for you to carry this ; you might lose it.

CHIP. That's why I want to find Miss Viola.

JAMESON. Well, she has gone off and will not be back for a week. I will take care of the will for you until she returns.

CHIP. But I jest saw her come into the house.

JAMESON. She went right out again and has gone into the country with the children. Here is some money to take care of yourself with until she returns. (Chip acts as though he would rather not take it.) I will let you know when she gets back.

CHIP. How will you know where to find me? Shall I call here?

JAMESON. No, you be round in front of the Astor House, a week from to-day. I will be there.

CHIP. You will keep the will all safe?

JAMESON. Yes.

CHIP. The will will be all right?

JAMESON. Yes, yes ; but come, you must be going, for the people that live here would not like to find you in the house.

CHIP You are Miss Viola's friend and the will will be all right? [Exit Chip at door.

JAMESON. (Hallooing after him.) Certainly. Turn to the left and keep right along. (Speaking to himself.) Jameson, you are in luck. Yes, there is money in it, and I'll do it, too. Yes, I will carry off the governess to some secluded place, and then, acting as her father, I will present the will, get the property, turn it into cash, and pocket it. (Suddenly, after a pause), By Jove! I have another idea. Enwright is as rich as a lord and thinks the world of his girl. I'll take her and Viola together, and get a reward out of him for her return. Then it will be thought that the governess has run off with the girl and no suspicion will be attached to me. It will be killing two birds with one stone. Jameson, old boy, I say again, you are in luck. I will not wait for the Lokers to put in their appearance, but be off at once to carry the idea into execution. The boy is disposed of all right and everything is lovely. Now for a fortune!

[Exit Jameson at door.

STREET DROP SCENE.

ACT II.

Scene Fifth. Street. Chip walking back and forth.

CHIP. Well, I'll be blowed! blest if I won't. New York is the darndest place I ever seed. Every one calls me country. I tell 'em that that ain't my name; that it is Chip Winkle, Esq. Then they laugh at me. Darn 'em, they don't know anything. I went up to the house, to-day, where I saw Miss Viola go in, to find out if she had got back, for the man that I give the will to has not been near the Castor Oil House as he promised; the consarned liar! The footman, anyway that's what the woman up there called him, kicked me out doors. (Puts hands behind him.) Asked the clerk of the Castor Oil House if there had been a man 'round in front of the house to see me; he kicked me out doors. (Puts hands behind him.) I'll get kicked next if I look at anybody.

[Enter Newsboy, L. 2 E.

NEWSBOY.—(Yells, as he enters), Here ye are, *Herald*, *Times*, *Tribune*, *World*, *Sun*, five o'clock edition; have a paper, country?

CHIP. That ain't my name; it's Chip Winkle, Esq.

NEWSBOY.—You don't say! Well, Squire, will ye have a paper?

CHIP. I don't care if I do.

[Newsboy gives him a paper.

CHIP. Thank ye.

NEWSBOY. No, ye don't! Give me two cents.

CHIP. Another New York trick. Ask a feller to have a paper and then charge him two cents for it. (Takes out an old pocketbook and gives him two big cents.) There goes two cents for nothin'; I've got to be more ecomical than this to live in New York.

NEWSBOY. (Going out, R. 2 E.) Tucked him! give him a last week's paper. He's greener than grass.

6

CHIP. (Opening paper, sits down and reads.) "Buffalos whitewash the Bostons." What in time did they whitewash 'em for? paint looks a darned sight better. "Great knock down in clothing." Gracious! I wish some one would knock me down some clothes. if it were'nt nothing more than a necktie. (Continues to look over paper, and all at once cries out), I'll be goll darned! here's a go. (Reads from paper in a blundering way. While reading Enwright enters and stands behind him.)

A GOVERNESS RUNS AWAY WITH A PUPIL!

FIVE THOUSAND DOLLARS REWARD!

The community will be startled to learn that the only child of the Hon. Edward Enwright, little Cora Enwright, was stolen from her home at Madam Loker's, last night, by her governess, Viola Wenley. No trace of the governess or child can be found. Enwright has only lately returned from Europe, and the loss of his child has nearly driven him crazy. The governess is tall, dark complected, with dark hair and eyes, of good form and pleasing manners. She is about eighteen years of age. The little girl is nine years old, light complected, and remarkably bright for one so young. Enwright offers five thousand dollars for any information that will lead to her recovery. The governess and child were greatly attached to each other, and why the governess should run off with her is a mystery.

CHIP. Well, of all the goll darned stories, that is the goll darnedest. Miss Viola would n't steal a pin. She steal a little gal she was takin' care of! It's a lie! I'd just like to hear some one say she would; I'd smash 'em so they would 'nt know themselfs. (Gets up and jumps about shaking his fists. Suddenly sees Enwright and stops.) Well, I'll be shot! Where'd ye come from?

ENWRIGHT. I have been here some time, my lad; you appear to know something about the case which you have been reading. I am Mr. Enwright; tell me what you know.

CHIP. (Excited.) Ye don't say ye are the man they tell about—the Hon. Edward Enwright?

ENWRIGHT. Yes, the same man.

CHIP. (Pulling off coat and doubling his fists and starting for him.) Then, by gosh, I'm goin' to lick ye, I'll be goll darned if I ain't. Come on! I'll learn ye to say Miss Viola stole your little gal. Come on, I say.

ENWRIGHT. Hold on, hold on, my lad; you are excited. I did not say she did; the papers say that.

CHIP. Did n't you tell the paper folks so?

ENWRIGHT. No. Now tell me what you know about the case. In the first place, who are you?

CHIP. (Pulling on coat.) Chip Winkle, Esq., from Wenley Farm up in New Hampshire, on the bank of the Minniewawar river.

ENWRIGHT. Ah, you are the boy that called at my aunt's to-day.

CHIP. Yes, if you mean the place where they kicked me, —histed me. Say, mister, is that the way they treat everybody in New York?

ENWRIGHT. (Laughing.) Not hardly. But what do you know about this case? How do you know this Miss Wenley would not carry off my little girl?

CHIP. Because she ain't that kind of a gal. I know her, I do. You see I use to live with her. She is the adopted child of Amos Wenley, who is dead. Betsey Smith turned her out doors after he was buried, and she come to New York.

ENWRIGHT. What's all this got to do about the case? Who's this Betsey Smith?

CHIP. Give me time and I'll tell ye what it has got to do with it. Betsey Smith is Betsey Smith, the housekeeper, and if you want to know anything more about her you will have to write up and ask Charles Bemis; he's got out a history of all the folks up our way. After Miss Viola came to New York, folks said there was another will. I found it after a while, and then I ups and cuts for New York. Got rides on stages, carts, anything I could; slept most anywhere, nights. Folks ask me where I was bound to, and give me my victuals. At last I got here, and after awhile I see Miss Viola on the street and followed her to yer aunt's. The footman wan't around the first time, so I didn't get kicked out. Found a tall, dark man in a room, nice room, I tell ye. I asked for Miss Viola and he said she had gone off into the country with the children, and would not be back for a week. I told him about the will, and he took it to keep, for he said he was a friend of Miss Viola's, and he was afraid I would lose it. He give me some money to take care of meself with until she got back, and told me he would see me at the Castor Oil House in a week.

ENWRIGHT. Astor House, you mean.

CHIP. Didn't ask her into any house. There wan't no her. Who said anything about asked her? I'm talking about a tarvern.

ENWRIGHT. Certainly, I understand. You called the Astor House the Castor Oil House, and I corrected you. You mistook Astor for asked her.

CHIP. Call me a thief, do ye? I never took anything in my life.

ENWRIGHT. What ideas you get into your head. I did not say you took anything, but that you thought I said asked her instead of Astor.

CHIP. Oh, that't it; well, Castor House.

ENWRIGHT. No, no, Astor House.

CHIP. Well, it is a house, anyway. Time come, but no man, and I went up to your aunt's to see him and got kicked out. (Puts hands behind him.) Then I asked for him at the hotel,—what ye call it?

ENWRIGHT. Astor House.

CHIP. Well, I got kicked out there. (Puts hands behind him.) It's kick, kick, kick. I tell ye that Miss Viola would never steal your little gal. No, sir, she would n't.

ENWRIGHT. (Aside.) I think the boy is right. The man he speaks of answers to Jameson. He has been away since the governess and Cora disappeared. Aunt said he was off on business, but it may be wrong, and he be at the bottom of the affair, after all. I'll take the boy up to the house and show him Jameson's picture, and see if he and the man that took the will are the same. If they are, and he would do as the boy says he has, he would be mean enough for anything. (Addressing Chip.) Here, boy, come with me, and see if you can tell your man by a picture; perhaps he is the guilty one in this case.

CHIP. All right!

[Exit Enwright and Chip, R. 2 E. Enter Jameson R. 1 E., smoking a cigar.

JAMESON. I thought I would take a run down to the city and see how things were working. Everything is lovely! Enwright has offered five thousand dollars' reward for his girl, but he has got to come up more than that. Wenley Farm is as good as mine; things could not work any better.

[Exit Jameson, L. 2 E. Enter Chip, on the run, R. 1 E.

CHIP. I saw him. It's the man that's got the will. I'll be darned if it ain't.

[Exit Chip, running, L. 2 E. Enter Enwright, R. 1 E.

ENWRIGHT. I wonder where that boy has gone to. He recognized the picture of Jameson as the man that took the will. Looking out of the window into the street, he saw some one, and thrusting the money I had given him to buy him some new clothes with, into his pocket, he started off as though he was crazy. What can it mean? I am satisfied that Jameson knows something about the governess and Cora being spirited away. I will set detectives on his track at once. The boy is after him to get the will and between us both he will stand a chance of being caught. I wonder where Chip Winkle, Esq., went to.   [Exit Enwright, L. 2 E.

ACT III.

Scene First.   Chamber.   Table and two Chairs.   Viola seated.   Cora has head in Viola's lap.

VIOLA.   Don't cry, Cora.

CORA.   I cannot help it; I wan't to see papa. Why are we kept locked up here in the woods by Mr. Jameson? Aunt said he was a good man; a good man would not do so.

VIOLA.   I don't know; but come, cheer up. It won't do any good to cry. God won't let him hurt us.

CORA.   I want to go home. Why does he keep us here?

VIOLA.   It is more than I can tell.

[Enter Jameson, in a rude manner, L. 2 E.

JAMESON.   (Throwing hat on floor.)   Well, I can tell you why you are kept here. It is for money; yes, money.

VIOLA.   I have no money, so that cannot be the reason for your conduct towards me. It may be in Cora's case. Such treatment is an outrage.

CORA.   (Going to Jameson.)   Please, sir, let us go.

JAMESON.   (Slapping Cora.)   Go sit down.

[Cora cries and sits down.

VIOLA.   (Arising.)   Don't you dare strike that child again. If your brutish nature demands that you must strike some one, strike me, but spare Cora.

JAMESON.   (Sneeringly.)   You ought to go on to the stage. Fact, I assure you.

VIOLA.   (Sitting down.)   Leave us!

JAMESON.   When I get ready. (Takes will from pocket and hands to Viola.)   You said you had no money. Read that and see.

VIOLA.   (Reading will.)   Why, it's a will; father's will, willing his property to me, his adopted daughter.

JAMESON.   Yes, and I am your father.

VIOLA.   What! you my father? Good God! can it be that such a villian as you are my father? Oh, would I had never known it. No, it cannot be. You are not my father.

JAMESON.   Since you have got your hand in at reading legal papers, just read that. (Draws paper from pocket and gives to Viola.)   It is a marriage certificate, and it proves that Mary Fernald, your mother, married me at Boston, Mass., July 4, 1863. The names, George Jameson and

Mary Fernald, are plain enough, ain't they? Do you wan't any more proof?

[Viola groans, drops paper and lays head on table.

JAMESON. (Taking will and certicate and putting them into his pocket.) Well, are you satisfied now that I am your father?

VIOLA. (In a low tone.) Yes.

JAMESON. So far, so good. Now, being your father, I propose to present the will and take possession of the property. To that end you will please sign this paper. (Takes paper, pocket ink-stand and pen-holder from his pocket and lays them on the table.) The paper gives me authority from you to take charge of the property. I can collect it without it, but it will be better to have it. Come, sign it.

VIOLA. I will not.

JAMESON. You won't eh? (Draws pistol and aims at her.) Sign that paper, if you care to live.

VIOLA. (Sneering.) You are a brave man, you are! Draw a pistol on a defenseless woman! How brave!

JAMESON. Shut up and sign.   [Viola finally signs.

JAMESON. There, you might as well have done so before. When I have realized the cash on the property you can go free; until then you are a prisoner. (Turns to Cora.) And when your father offers a big enough reward for you, you can go free, and not until then. (Turns to Viola.) Perhaps you would like to know where you are. Well, you are confined in an old farm house just south of Wenley Farm.

VIOLA. Wenley Farm?

JAMESON. Yes, there is nothing like being near the scene of action. Then, again, no one would think of looking here. A place nearer New York would be searched. Farewell.

[Exit Jameson at door.

VIOLA. The villain!

CORA. Papa, will save us yet.

VIOLA. I pray to God he may.

FOREST DROP SCENE.

ACT III.

Scene Second.   Forest.

[Enter Jameson L. 2 E., drunk.

JAMESON. (Hiccoughs.) Well, I've done it—told 'em everything. (Hiccoughs.) The darn girls kinder upset me. (Hiccoughs.) I've been through enough, I thought, to face 'em, but I sware, it took a considerable liquor to brace me up for it. (Hiccoughs.) It did, and when I got through telling 'em what's wnat, it took more to settle my nerves.

Jameson, what's the matter with you? (Hiccoughs.) I give
it to the girls, straight, anyway, without any fooling. (Hiccoughs.) Feel kinder queer. Quite a forest about the place.
Couldn't got a better house to put my prisoners. (Hiccoughs.) Darn it all! What's the matter with me? I ain't
drunk. Who says I'm drunk? (Hiccoughs.) I feel (hiccoughs) just as good as they frame 'em. (Hiccoughs and
falls down.) I'm all right!   [Enter Chip, L. 2 E.

CHIP. I'll be goll darned if I ain't gettin' to be quite a
traveler. From New Hampshire to New York and from New
York to New Hampshire! Wonder how my name would
sound wrote "Chip Winkle, Esq., great American traveler."
(Pause.) Gosh! it sounds like thunder; the addition spoils
the effect of the "Esq." I'll be blest if I'll change it. That
'ere feller that's got the will has give me a big old chase.
When I sees him in New York I followed him to the depot;
he got a ticket for Marlborough. I took the money Mr.
Enwright give me to get some clothes, and got a ticket, too,
and here I am. He's here in the woods somewhere, for I
tracked him to the edge of 'em; I'll find him. (Suddenly
sees Jameson on the ground.) By gosh all hemlock! If
there ain't the goll darned sardine now. (Stepping up and
looking at him.) He's asleep. Wonder if he's got the will
about him. (Opening his coat.) I'll find out. Whew, I
guess he and Deacon Cuff have gone in together a-killing
potato bugs. Kill 'em to get near enough to smell his breath.
(Takes will out of pocket and looks at it.) Hurrah! it's the
stolen will. Gracious, I've woke him up; I'll dodge behind
a tree until he gets out of the way.   [Exit Chip, L. 3 E.

JAMESON. (Getting up.) Thought I heard some one speak.
Guess I've been asleep and got to dreaming; head feels like
a bushel basket. (Gags.) I must get along; got to see to
gals.   [Exit, staggering, R. 2 E.   Enter Chip, L. 3 E.

CHIP. By gosh! you are caught. "Got to see to the gals,"
eh? Well, I'll jest foller up and see where they be. I've got
the will, and now all that's wanted is to find Viola and Cora.
Then Chip Winkle, Esq., will settle down to work again.
       [Exit Chip, R. 2 E.   Enter Deacon Cuff, R. 1 E.

DEACON. Wonder who that man and boy were. I didn't
get a square look at the lad, but seems to me I've seen him
before. Well, well, what's all this got to do about my popping the question to Betsey Smith? My dear, departed
Lorilla (wipes his eyes) has been dead nearly three years now.
A man of my standing in society,—deacon of the orthodox
church and president of the town reform club, should surely
take to himself a wife. I'd popped before, but Betsey keeps

a turning the subject when I get started to. I'll call upon her at once. Before going I'll take a little drink for my health ; doctor says my system is out of order ; I need something to build me up—a little ardent as a medicine is a good thing. (Takes out pint bottle and drinks.) I must hide the bottle afore I call on Betsey, she is so sensitive. (Takes another drink ; puts bottle in pocket.) Remarkable nice woman, though.

[Exit, L. 2 E.

(Fire looms up in the distance at right. Cries of fire outside. Farmers and firemen run by, farmers with pails, hoes and shovels. Enwright goes through with the rest. All cry " fire !")

RAISE FOREST DROP SCENE.

ACT III.

Scene Third. Kitchen of Wenley Farmhouse. Betsey Smith chopping pie meat. Deacon Cuff churning butter.

DEACON. (Churning.) The butter is coming.

BETSEY. (Chopping.) All right ; I'll 'tend to it in jest a minute.

DEACON. It 's come.

BETSEY. Churn it a little more ; it makes the butter better. I'll jest carry this mince meat out and put it in the buttery and be right back. [Exit Betsey, L. 2 E.

DEACON. I'm going to pop the question. Lucky I didn't hide that medicine as I intended to. (Takes a drink, puts bottle back.) I was crazy to think of hiding it, in my state of health. She set me to churning just as soon as I got here. I 'll pop anyway. [Enter Betsey, L. 2 E.

BETSEY. (Aside.) So he 's going to pop, is he? The old fool, to think I 'd marry him. If I knew for sure he had not got that will, I 'd pop him out of here in a hurry. (Addressing Deacon and looking into churn.) There, that will do ; thank you, I'm glad you called, for it 's hard for me to churn.

DEACON. You should have some one to do your churning for you.

BETSEY. Yes, I 've got to hire some one. I should have done so before, but I reckoned that that Chip would turn up.

DEACON. Why hire? Betsey, there are many who would make you a good husband.

BETSEY. (Aside.) I must cut him off before he pops. I don't want to mad him, and it would to refuse him. I ought to burnt that will up and then I would not have had all this trouble. (Addressing deacon.) Deacon, will you please carry the churn out to the dairy? I always work the butter over there.

DEACON. Why, certainly.

[Exit deacon, with churn, R. 2 E.

BETSEY. The old fool!

[Betsey busies herself about the room. Enter Deacon, R. 2 E.

DEACON. I carried it down.

BETSEY. Thank you.

DEACON. As I was remarking, you should get—

BETSEY. (Interrupting.) I am going to get a hired man.

DEACON. No, no, I meant to say that you should get married. I am president of the town reform club and deacon of the Orthodox church, and—

BETSEY. (Interrupting.) Yes, yes, you are a very prominent man, Deacon.

DEACON. A man in my position should take to himself a wife.

BETSEY. Certainly.

DEACON. I have made up my mind to do so.

BETSEY. I am pleased to hear you say so. Nancy Brown has been dying for you this two years; she will make you a good wife.

DEACON. It is not Nancy Brown I have decided to take.

BETSEY. (Interrupting.) Oh, it's Hannah Mason.

DEACON. Why, no. Let me—

BETSEY. Of course you can. (Takes out snuff box and passes it.) Take a pinch; it's the best old Maccaboy.

DEACON. (Taking pinch of snuff.) I was not about to ask for a pinch of snuff, as you supposed, although it is acceptable. You are too hasty—jump at conclusions. Have you—

BETSEY. (Interrupting.) Yes, I've a bean in my snuff to give it flavor. It is a West India bean; one of the best.

DEACON. Betsey, I really wish you would not interrupt so. I have long thought a great deal of you. Poor, dear, departed Lorilla has been dead nearly three years, and it becomes a man of my standing in society to take to himself a wife; as I was about to remark when you spoke, have you not noticed—(Sneezes long and loud.) Pretty powerful snuff. To continue; have you not noticed that you occupy a place in my feelings (Sneezes) that none but you can fill. (Sneezes and wig falls off.) What, what! (Sneezing and putting wig back on in great haste.) Terrible powerful snuff, that.

BETSEY. (Aside.) The bald headed sinner! (Addressing deacon.) Yes, the old Maccaboy seems to raise the old boy.

DEACON. (Surprised.) Such talk is unbecoming a lady of your years; it really is.

BETSEY. You looked so funny I couldn't help it. Excuse

7

me, Deacon. (Aside.) It won't do to get him mad. How I wish I had burnt that will.

DEACON. (Aside.) Perhaps she will talk to me like that when she gets to be Mrs. Deacon Cuff. I'll excuse it for now. (Addressing Betsey and feeling to see if wig is all right.) Certainly, certainly. As I was about to remark—
[Rap at door.

DEACON. I bet it is John after me. The old mare had the belly-ache this morning, before I came away, and I should n't wonder a bit if she had another attack. What trials a man of property does have.   [Rap at door, louder than before.

BETSEY. Come in.   [Enter Enwright at door.

ENWRIGHT. Excuse me for intruding. There has been a fire on the hill.

BETSEY. Been a fire?

DEACON. You don't say so!

ENWRIGHT. Yes, a young lady and my daughter just escaped with their lives. Can we stop here until teams can be got to take us to the village?

BETSEY. Why, yes, you can stop for a while. I am a lone, poor woman, and of course you will give me a little something for the trouble.

ENWRIGHT. (Aside.) The old miser   (Addressing Betsey.) Certainly.

DEACON. Have you got any teams yet?

ENWRIGHT. No.

DEACON. Well, I'll carry you down. I've got the best mare in Marlborough. I'm Deacon Cuff. Probably you have seen my name in the papers for I'm president of the town reform club and deacon of the Orthodox church. I'll carry you cheap.

ENWRIGHT. I do not know as I ever heard of you; you may consider yourself engaged, though. Get a team ready as soon as you can. (Addressing Betsey.) I will return with the party at once.   [Exit Enwright at door.

DEACON. (Putting on hat.) As I was saying—

BETSEY. (Interrupting.) Well, well, never mind now; you have got to get your team ready.

DEACON. (Going out at door, while Betsey arranges things about the room.) Yes, yes. (Gets partly out of the door and takes out bottle and drinks.) My system requires a little stimulant. (Puts bottle in pocket and turns around and cries back to Betsey) Good bye!

BETSEY. Good day. (Aside.) The old fool. (Pause.) It's just a year ago to-night since Viola went away. I read in the *Herald* a week or two ago that she had run away with a little girl where she had been teaching, and that no trace of her could be found. I always knew that no good would come of that Mary Fernald's brat. I'd just like to know where Chip went to. The will was missing about the time he went off, but he would not have taken it. He's too big a fool for that. The deacon has got it fast enough. Strange how the appearance of that stranger set me to thinking.

[Noise outside. Enter at door, Enwright, carrying Viola in his arms, Chip with Cora in his arms. Viola is in a dead faint.

BETSEY. (Surprised.) The Lord save us! It's Viola and Chip.

[Enwright lays Viola on settee. Chip sets Cora down.

• CHIP. This is Wenley Farm.

VIOLA. (Coming to.) Where am I? Is Cora safe? What has happened?

CHIP. Everything is correct!

ENWRIGHT. You are at what Chip calls Wenley Farm. Cora is safe, thanks to your courage and Chip's bravery. The house where you were held a prisoner with Cora caught fire by accident. I got there just in time to see Chip lowering you from a chamber window. You look surprised at this. Well, it is a long story. Chip came to New York in search of you and found where you were only to hear that you had kidnapped Cora, as it was then thought. I met him, and through him you were found, for he stood up so strong in your favor I was led to believe you innocent, and for various reasons caused· to mistrust a man named Jameson—George Jameson. I gave Chip some money to get him some clothes, for he was sadly in need of them, and was about to enter into an extended conversation with him, when he left like a flash. It was found he had followed some one to Marlborough, and judging it to be Jameson, I started on after him.

CHIP. That's so, every time, Miss Viola. I come to New York to hunt ye up and tell ye that Betsey Smith (Looks at Betsey) stole Mr. Wenley's last will and put one he made before in place of it. Here's the will. (Takes will from pocket and gives it Viola who gets up and reads it.) The man Jameson stole it from me ; he said he was yer friend and took it to keep for ye. I found him asleep, out doors, drunk, and stole it back. 'Bout as soon as I got it, he woke up and started on ; I after him like a picked up dinner. Wall, he stopped at the place where he had ye and Cora, and about that time the fire broke out. I knew the house like a book — use to hunt bats in it, for nobody use to live there—and I soon got into ye room where ye was and got ye out. (Nodding to Enwright.) He's 'lated the rest

BETSEY. (Screams.) Everything is lost! What shall I do?

CHIP. Go shoot yourself! That's the best thing for such an old tarnal as ye are.

CORA. ·You should not talk so.

VIOLA. Cora is right, Chip.

CHIP. She is an old tarnal, anyway. Did n't she make me work like a nigger? did n't she turn you out doors? did'nt she steal the will? Darn her!

ENWRIGHT. She has done wrong, Chip, but for all that you should not talk so.

CHIP. Well, I hate her, I do.

BETSEY. Oh, dear; oh, dear; what shall I do? I 've been an awful woman. I 'll kill myself.

[Starts to go out at door, but runs against Jameson, who reels in, appearances indicating that he has been through a fire. Jameson sinks on to settee.

JAMESON. (Gasping.) I am burning up. Curse it, how I burn! My life is come to an end. What a life it has been! I 'll not die until I do what I can to set myself right. (Rises up.) Viola, come nearer. (She does so and he sinks back.) I am dying, but I cannot die until I confess to you. I escaped from the burning building and followed you here as fast as I could in my feeble condition. I told you once I was your father and showed you a certificate to prove it. 'T was a lie; I am not your father; he was killed by me in a fight over seventeen years ago. My true name is John Stanley. The officers were on my track for relieving a bank of its cash, and the idea struck me of putting myself in his place, that is, making it appear so. I resembled him greatly, and changing clothes and disguising myself slightly, John Stanley was dead and George Jameson lived, as far as the world knew. The certificate was in the pocket of his coat. Not daring to trust to your mother being deceived, I kept away from her, and she died broken hearted, thinking she was deserted. So she was, by death. I 've been a deep villain. It was I that murdered Amos Wenley, God forgive me? (Rises up and laughs in a wild manner.) Curse it, how I burn! Fire! fire! fire! How it blazes! [Falls back dead.

VIOLA. He is dead. What a life he has led! May God have mercy on his soul!

ENWRIGHT. Amen!

BETSEY. Would that I were dead too!

[Enter Sheriff at door, with Constable.

OFFICER. We are in search of one George Jameson. He is charged with murder and robbery; he was seen to enter here.

ENWRIGHT. (Pointing to settee.) There he is, but he is beyond the reach of human law ; gone to that high tribunal before which we must all appear. Take him away and see that he is buried. I will bear the expense.

[Officers go out at door with body, Enwright, Viola and Cora stand in a group together, talking in low tones.

CHIP. (Aside.) Kind of a family pow-wow, I reckon. (Addressing Betsey.) Well, what do ye think?

BETSEY. (Crying.) I've been an awful bad woman.

CHIP. No need of tellin' of it ; everybody knew it before.

BETSEY. I wish I was dead !

CHIP. Die, then. Your funeral procession won't be very long.

VIOLA. (Reproachfully.) Chip! (Addressing Betsey.) Betsey Smith, you have been a bold, bad woman, but I cannot find it in my heart to punish you. While you live you are welcome to a home here ; I will never expose you. I am going back to New York to live (Chip whistles) and shall come once a year to visit the old place and the graveyard on the hill. Try to atone for your past life in the years to come.

BETSEY. The Lord bless you. I don't deserve it. You are too good.

CHIP. Well, I'll be goll darned ! Goin' to be a governess and give the place up ! And to Betsey Smith, too.

ENWRIGHT. You look surprised. Viola is going back to New York, not as governess, but as my wife. It's all settled.

CHIP. I vum ! Ye don't say so, do ye?

ENWRIGHT. Yes. Chip, you have been a good and faithful fellow, and you shall go with us. The reward of five thousand dollars I offered for the recovery of Cora is yours, and shall be placed in the bank to your credit at once.

[Enwright, Viola, R., Cora, C., Betsey, Chip, L.

CHIP. Well, I'll be goll darned ! who'd ha' thought all this would ha' happened just 'cause of " The Stolen Will? "

FRONT CURTAIN.